WISHING STAR SUMMER

by Beryl Young

RAINCOAST BOOKS

Vancouver

Raincoast Books acknowledges the ongoing support of the Canada Council; the British Columbia Ministry of Small Business, Tourism and Culture through the B.C. Arts Council; and the Government of Canada through the Book Publishing Industry Development Program (BPIDP).

First published in 2001 by
Raincoast Books
9050 Shaughnessy Street
Vancouver, B.C.
V6P 6E5
(604) 323-7100
www.raincoast.com

Edited by Joy Gugeler
Typeset by Bamboo & Silk Design Inc.
Cover art by Julia Bell

2 3 4 5 6 7 8 9 10

NATIONAL LIBRARY OF CANADA CATALOGUING IN PUBLICATION DATA
    Young, Beryl, 1934-
    Wishing star summer
    ISBN 1-55192-450-1
    I. Title.
    PS8597.O575W57 2001   jC813'.6   C2001-910180-5
    PZ7.Y846Wi 2001

At Raincoast Books we are committed to protecting the environment and to the responsible use of natural resources. We are acting on this commitment by working with suppliers and printers to phase out our use of paper produced from ancient forests — this book is one step towards that goal. It is printed on 100% ancient-forest-free paper (100% recycled, 40% post-consumer), processed chlorine-free, and supplied by New Leaf Paper; it is printed with vegetable-based inks by Webcom. For further information, visit our website at www.raincoast.com. We are working with Markets Initiative (www.oldgrowthfree.com) on this project.

Printed and bound in Canada by Webcom

To Brian, Deanne, Cameron and Emily,
with thanks

CONTENTS

ONE

What do you do when you're a perfectly okay eleven year old and none of the girls at your new school can stand you?

Well, Jillian told herself, *you walk right past them down the hall, look straight ahead and pretend you don't care. You unzip your dripping jacket and throw it on the bottom of your locker. Don't pick it up. Don't look around.*

Jillian grabbed her science book from the shelf, banged the locker door shut, snapped the lock and marched into the classroom to begin another painful day in 6B.

She dropped into her seat, shivered and pushed her rain-soaked hair behind her ears. "I hate this stupid school," she muttered through pinched lips.

Kids were rustling papers and shifting books; the smell of wet runners drifted around the room. Outside it was still raining. Coming to Vancouver in the middle of the school year had been a big mistake.

"You'll like 6B," the vice-principal had told Jillian and her mother that first week in February. "It's a friendly class and Ms. Kaminsky is an excellent teacher."

Right about the teacher. Wrong about the class.

Some of the boys were friendly enough, especially Ross, who wore his black baseball cap backward and knew the difference between a minotaur and a griffin, but making friends with the 6B girls? Impossible! Other than handing out money, Jillian hadn't thought of a way to win them over.

Last week, after being ignored for a whole month, she'd braved the corner of the playground where Gail, Molly, Nevea and Jasmine hung out. They'd stopped talking and stared at her, which made Jillian stumble over her words. "I was, ah, wondering why we don't have French here until grade seven? In Ottawa we, ah, started French in grade one."

"Parlay-voo? Come-on-tally vous?" Molly sing-songed through a mouthful of glinting braces.

"How's your Chinese?" Gail said, tossing her head to a chorus of tittering girls.

Jillian had pretended to laugh too, but she knew an insult when she heard one and she hadn't stuck around. She would never be part of that group. Never. She'd walked across the playground to the boys' soccer field where Ross waved, but nobody else paid any attention to her.

She shouldn't have mentioned French, even if it was

an official language. In Vancouver, kids spoke all kinds of languages. Gail's family had come from China when Gail was four years old. Nevea was from Honduras and Jasmine had been born in Vancouver after her parents emigrated from the Punjab. They'd probably thought Jillian was boasting when she talked about learning French in grade one. But what *could* she talk about? Her cat? Her annoying brother? The yucky weather?

Jasmine was the girl Jillian really wanted for a friend. Jasmine wasn't mean like Gail and Molly. She wore tiny sparkling diamonds in each ear and had thick, dark hair that bounced over her shoulders, unlike Jillian's hair, which was plain brown and hung straight down.

Jasmine had at least stopped to say hello in the hall one day, which had been just the encouragement Jillian needed to ask if she'd come over after school.

Jasmine's brown eyes had been friendly, but she'd said, "Sorry, I've got a piano lesson."

Jillian's legs had been weak as she watched Jasmine disappear around the corner. *Was the lesson just an excuse?*

Now it was March and Jasmine had given out invitations for her birthday party this Friday. The party was all the girls could talk about and Jillian wasn't invited.

"Jasmine's birthday tonight will be great," Molly had said that morning. "We'll paint pots at the ceramics studio, then go back to Jasmine's for a sleepover."

"That's so-o-o cool," Gail squealed.

Jillian knew what was wrong. She didn't know *how* to make friends. In Ottawa, she'd always *had* friends, kids she'd known since kindergarten. Here she'd spent many lunch hours watching the younger kids in the playground, but today she'd decided to go back in the classroom to read. Ms. Kaminsky lifted her head from the papers she was marking and gave Jillian a concerned look.

"Everything alright, Jillian?"

"Yes. Fine."

She would have liked to talk to Ms. Kaminsky about it, but a teacher would probably say something to the girls and then they'd hate her even more.

The bell went and the kids tramped noisily back into the room. As Molly and Gail took their seats they looked over at Jillian, laughing behind their hands, "Teacher's pet."

Jillian was furious, but kept her head down and pretended she hadn't heard.

"Not hungry, Jillian?" her mother asked that night at supper.

"Nope," Jillian answered.

Jillian's dad looked at her and leaned over to tip up her chin. "Things okay at school?"

"The same as ever."

"What does that mean?" asked her mother.

"THE SAME!" Jillian slammed down her fork. "None of the kids talk to me at lunch or recess. I might as well be invisible."

"You're still new at school. They'll get to know you soon," her father said sympathetically.

"They just don't like me. When I hear them laughing, I know they're laughing at *me*."

"Why not invite someone over after school?" Jillian's dad suggested.

"I already did. I asked Jasmine and she said no. There's no one else to ask, except Ross, and a girl can't ask a *boy* over."

David sighed. "A boy can't ask a girl either," he said in a scratchy voice. "Unless you're like most of the boys here who already have girlfriends. I'm over the hill at fifteen."

Mrs. Nelson put down her glass. "And I'm still unemployed. I'm tired of pounding the streets with my portfolio when there are no mediation jobs in this city. I never thought it would be so hard to find work."

Jillian glared at her father. "See what you did when you made us leave Ottawa for your stupid job!"

"Jillian!" her mother scolded, her blond ponytail flipping from side to side.

"Well," Mr. Nelson said, "it may be stupid but it's the best job of my career. And moving here was a family decision, remember? I thought all of us were pleased to be living near Gram and to have the ocean and mountains on our doorstep."

"What mountains?" David asked. "It rains so much we can't even see them. They don't call this the Wet Coast for nothing."

"Why am I the only person in this family who feels

happy about the move?" Mr. Nelson said, running his fingers through his hair to check if it was getting thin on top.

On the way upstairs to her room, Jillian remembered how much she'd liked the new house when she first saw it. It sat at the top of a small hill and had wide steps leading up to the front door.

"In the summer we'll be able to sit here and see the whole world," her dad had said.

Jillian's bedroom had a window seat that looked over the back garden. She gazed around the room, checking her collection of books, CDs and stuffed animals on the bookshelf. Two pictures of woodland fairies hung on the wall and a red music box sat on the dresser.

Chester, the tortoiseshell cat they'd found at the SPCA right after they'd arrived, sat on the window seat and was putting his paw up to the glass to trace the path of each raindrop as it rolled down the dark window.

Jillian reached out to hug her cat. "It's never going to stop raining, Chester. I'd like to pack you up and go back to Ottawa."

At this very minute the girls in 6B were at Jasmine's sleepover. They'd be talking all night, talking about *her*. Jillian felt tears sting her eyes and she rubbed her face against Chester's fur.

When her mother came in to say good night she tucked Jillian into bed and sat down beside her.

Jillian sighed. "I just can't figure out why the kids at

school don't like me. I try to be friendly, I wear the same clothes as the other girls and I don't rat to the teacher when they're mean. The only person in 6B who likes me *is* the teacher."

"Give it time, Jillian," her mother said as she kissed her daughter's cheek. "Off to sleep now."

Jillian pulled up the quilt and placed her warm cat across her chest, his paws splayed on her shoulders. She felt the steady wave of Chester's purring, put her cheek close to his ear with the question she was too ashamed to ask anyone else.

Why didn't Jasmine invite me to her birthday party?

"The best party ever!" Molly cooed as Jillian approached the lockers.

"It was so-o-o cool!" Gail squeaked as they entered the classroom.

Jillian kicked her locker door shut and clenched her jaw so hard it hurt — the start of another Monday morning.

"Settle down please, class," Ms. Kaminsky said. "Language Arts this morning. You'll see a new vocabulary list on the blackboard. Please use each word in a sentence."

Twenty minutes later she called on students to read what they'd written.

"Ross, please use the word 'received' in a sentence."

"In the middle of the night I received a message from outer space."

The class laughed and Ms. Kaminsky continued down the list until she got to the last word. "Jillian, please use the word 'ignorant' in a sentence."

Jillian took a big breath and leaned an elbow on the notebook in front of her. In a clear, strong voice, she read, "The girls in 6B are ignorant."

The entire class was silent and Ms. Kaminsky looked shocked. Jillian's face burned. For the rest of the morning she felt the weight of Ms. Kaminsky's disapproval and avoided looking at her.

Jillian was the first person out of the room when the bell rang. She grabbed her lunch and sat in the lunchroom at a table by herself. Only the primary children came to join her. She gave half her tuna sandwich to a freckled boy who was always hungry and her cookie to a shy girl who never talked to anyone. On the playground, the little kids followed Jillian around until they'd all had a push on the swings.

In the afternoon Ms. Kaminsky announced the beginning of their science unit on electricity.

"The world today has an ever-expanding need for electricity," she said, "and that need is increasingly being met with nuclear power. There are now over four hundred nuclear power plants around the world. In Canada alone we have fourteen, and with each new plant the risk of nuclear accidents increases."

"In 1986," she went on, "there was a horrible accident at a large nuclear power plant at Chernobyl in the

Ukraine. The explosion blew radioactive dust into the air and, because of the direction of the wind that day, seventy per cent of it fell on the neighbouring country of Belarus, just ten kilometres away."

The class listened intently. Ms. Kaminsky walked over to the globe on the corner table. "We're here in Vancouver," she said, running her finger across the blue Atlantic Ocean and turning the globe halfway around. "And here is Belarus, a small country in eastern Europe bordering Poland, Russia and the Ukraine."

"What caused the accident at Chernobyl?" Jasmine asked.

Ms. Kaminsky explained that in the early morning of April 26, an employee failed to perform a safety check at one reactor. It overheated and exploded, sending radioactive strontium, cesium and iodine into the air.

"One hundred times more radioactivity than all the world's nuclear tests put together," she said gravely.

The students were quiet.

"Because of the accident, much of the soil and water in Belarus will be contaminated for hundreds of years."

Ms. Kaminsky sat back on the edge of her desk. "Almost all the children in Belarus, even those not born at the time of the explosion, are continually exposed to radiation and have weak immune systems."

Ross put up his hand to ask a question. "Does a weak immune system mean they're going to die?"

"The children get very tired and, if they get a cold or flu, it takes them a long time to recover. Some of the children become sick with thyroid cancer or leukaemia. And, yes, some do die." Ms. Kaminsky paused before continuing, "Here's some good news. People in twenty-seven countries around the world invite Belarusian children for health respite visits. In Canada, an organization based in Ottawa arranges summer visits for more than four hundred children a year.

"But why would they come to Canada?" Molly asked.

"Because we have clean air and water and healthy food. We can also give the children medical and dental treatments they can't get at home," Ms. Kaminsky answered.

When the bell rang, Jillian and Ross left the school-yard together. The rain had stopped and a sliver of sun came through the thin clouds, warming the spring air.

"I don't think there should be any nuclear power plants," Ross said as they walked along the street.

"I don't either," Jillian said. "Imagine what it would be like to live in Belarus. It makes me feel lucky to be born in Canada. Hey, that gives me an idea …"

"I know what you're going to say, but I can't invite a kid to stay 'cause I'll be in Winnipeg with my dad for the summer."

They walked past the apartment building where Ross lived.

"I'm glad you're still talking to me," Jillian said. "I guess what I said in class about the girls wasn't fair."

"Not too bright either," said Ross. "Anyway, just

'cause someone makes a mistake doesn't mean I stop talking to them." Ross adjusted his baseball cap. "I've been known to make a mistake now and then myself." Sheepishly, he turned around to walk back to his apartment.

Jillian laughed and continued up the hill.

It wasn't going to be much of a summer with no one but Chester for company, but if her family invited a girl from Belarus she'd be *guaranteed* a friend.

Yes! A girl to bike with, to take to the beach, to share secrets! She started to run. She'd break the news at the dinner table, tell them about the poor Belarus children, their contaminated food, their weak immune systems. By the time she brought up the idea of the Nelson family hosting a girl, she'd have won her parents over. Yes!

TWO

W hat do you do when you have a perfectly good plan, but you need to convince your family to go along with it?

You start at the beginning and you go slowly.

Jillian hopped from one foot to the other as she helped her mother with dinner. She tossed down the cutlery, smacked the salad bowl onto the table and shoved David into his chair. Before she was in her own seat she burst out, "We've got to invite a girl from Belarus to live with us!"

"Tell me you're joking!" David said.

"Sit down, Jillian," her dad said.

"What's a Belarus anyway?" David asked.

"It's a country," Jillian answered, but still the words spilled out too quickly. "Ms. Kaminsky said it used to be part of the USSR. In 1986 there was a nuclear explosion and a huge cloud of radioactive dust blew over Belarus."

"The world's worst nuclear accident," her mother added.

"We have to *do* something," Jillian said. "Kids are being poisoned."

"You're exaggerating," David said, helping himself to salad.

"Just a minute, now," Mr. Nelson said. "I remember the news reports about Chernobyl. A quarter of the land was contaminated and thousands of people had to be evacuated."

"Yes!" Jillian rushed on, encouraged that her parents were on her side. "I say we invite a girl from Belarus over here this summer so that she can get healthy."

"No way!" David said. "One girl in the house is enough."

"Hold it, David," said Mrs. Nelson.

"It's a kind idea, Jillian," said her dad, "but we've just moved in. The paint's hardly dry."

Jillian raised her voice. "The spare room next to mine is empty. She could sleep right there!" Jillian grabbed her father's arm and sent the basket of bread flying.

"Jillian, I use that room for sewing," her mother said firmly. "Now please drop the idea and pick up the bread."

Jillian lifted her arms, waving them like an orchestra conductor over the supper table. "Look at all this good food! When I think of those children eating contaminated meat and vegetables ..."

Open-mouthed, the family stared at Jillian, who

was extremely pleased to see she had their full attention.

"You probably think I'm being selfish, that I only want company for the summer, but this is not just something *I* want. This could be a matter of life and death."

The family continued to stare at Jillian.

"It's our *duty* to sponsor someone."

Mrs. Nelson shook her head. "Duty or not, Jillian, it just won't work."

"But we're not going anywhere this summer."

"If I ever get a job, I thought you'd like to go to camp," her mother said.

"I don't want to go to camp. I want to have a girl from Belarus right here in our house."

"Jillian, that's enough. Leave it alone!" Irritated, Mrs. Nelson headed for the kitchen.

Jillian stood up and flung her chair back so forcefully it crashed onto the floor. "This family is completely heartless!"

"Calm down, Jillian," her dad said, looking serious. "Now tell me the real reason you want this so badly."

"You want me to tell you? Fine, I'll tell you!" Jillian shouted, banging both fists on the table. "I haven't got one single friend at school. Not one." Her voice began to tremble. "I *desperately* need someone to hang out with this summer." She clenched her hands in front of her and closed her eyes.

"And the Academy Award goes to … Jillian Nelson," David said, getting up and leaving the room.

Jillian yelled after him. "I bet the girls call you a butter-brain with all that hair gel!"

"Come here, Jillian," said her dad, settling her on his knee. Jillian buried her head in the hollow between her father's shoulder and his neck, snuffling into the familiar smell of his shirt.

"I'll have an awful summer if we don't invite a girl to live with us, Dad," Jillian said.

"I'm beginning to think you may be right," said her father thoughtfully.

Jillian reached for the music box on the dresser and curled up on her bedroom window seat. She ran her fingers over the red velvet top and the border of gold braid. Grandpa had given her the music box for her third birthday and less than a year later he had died. Many times her mother and Gram had told Jillian how she sat on her grandfather's knee in a blue birthday dress while he showed her how to wind the key. Sadly, Jillian couldn't remember what her grandpa looked like or how it had felt to be with him. He was never more than a shadowy memory in the back of her mind.

She turned the key on the side of the box, the lid opened and a tiny fairy on a red velvet platform swung up as the wistful music began.

When you wish upon a star,
Makes no difference who you are,
Anything your heart desires
will come to you.

The delicate china fairy, the size of Jillian's little finger, pirouetted to the music. The fairy stood on tip-toe, one tiny arm curled in front like a dancer; the other in the air holding a wand topped with a sparkling silver star. It was the most exquisite thing Jillian owned. The fairy's eyes were blue, her mouth a dainty rosebud. She wore a short dress of mauve lily petals and her blond hair, entwined with blue forget-me-nots, cascaded over her shoulders. Best of all, the fairy had two gossamer wings of soft grey silk, each adorned with smoky circles like the marks on a butterfly.

Anything your heart desires will come to you …

Jillian knew what her heart desired. She fixed her eyes on the twirling silver star and made a wish.

Two days later Jillian sat at the breakfast table, picking at her scrambled eggs. David made himself a fourth piece of toast and Mr. Nelson poured more coffee.

Mrs. Nelson looked across the table at Jillian and David.

"Dad and I had a long talk last night. It's been a frustrating few months for me and I've decided to stop looking for a job until September. I shouldn't have said I need the spare room for sewing. That's not important."

Jillian held her breath.

"Maybe it would be a good idea for us to invite a child from Belarus this summer."

"Really?" Jillian asked, her eyes opening wide.

"Really?" David said, in mock horror.

"Really," their father answered with a smile.

"Awesome!" Jillian beamed and reached over to hug first her mother, then her father and then, to his great surprise, David.

"Watch it. You almost rammed the toast down my throat," he said.

"Hold on, Jillian. We're not there yet," her father cautioned. "We need to ask Ms. Kaminsky about contacting the Vancouver committee. They'll send someone to see if we're suitable."

"What? A test?" Jillian said.

David adopted a radio announcer's voice. "An indepth investigation has revealed that a strange eleven-year-old girl in the Nelson family has made them unsuitable for sponsorship …"

Jillian glared at her brother.

"You know," said their mother, "eight weeks is a long time. This will be a big commitment. If things get tough, we can't send the child home halfway through the summer."

"Okay, okay. I get it," said Jillian, shuffling impatiently. "Let's go for it. And when you phone, please ask for a girl about eleven."

Gram was over to play rummy when Sharon Skene, the volunteer from the committee, came for the home visit. Sharon was about the same age as Jillian's parents. She was tall, had curly auburn hair and wore purple-rimmed glasses. Jillian led her to the nicest chair in the living room and the Nelsons found seats around her. Sharon adjusted her glasses, smiled and told them she'd been an exchange student to Belarus about fifteen years ago.

"I have no family of my own so I've been volunteering with the Vancouver committee since the first children came over in 1991," Sharon said.

"What can you tell us about the organization?" Mrs. Nelson said.

"The Canadian Relief Fund for Chernobyl Victims assists local groups across the country in planning children's summer visits. It also brings Belarusian doctors to Canada to study treatments for radiation exposure and it sends medical equipment to Belarus."

"We really want to have a girl from Belarus live with us this summer," Jillian said.

"Wonderful," Sharon said. "If she comes, have you got a room for her?"

Jillian took Sharon upstairs to the spare bedroom.

"We'll fix it up," Jillian said nervously.

"Everything looks just fine," Sharon said.

Over a cup of tea Sharon gave them more background. "Belarus is almost the same latitude as Vancouver and has weather like Vancouver's in the summer, though in the winter it's more like eastern Canada."

"You mean snow, instead of rain. Like Ottawa, right?" Jillian asked.

"Right," said Sharon. "But Belarus is a small country, just ten million people, one third the population of Canada. Despite their size, their culture is very rich. The famous artist Marc Chagall was from Belarus.

And everyone knows Wayne Gretzky; his family came from Belarus too."

"I didn't know that," David said, "but when I was searching the Internet I found out that Belarusian gymnasts have won lots of gold medals at the Olympics."

Sharon nodded. "We sponsor children from the town of Chaussy in the south-east region of Mahilou, one of the areas most contaminated by Chernobyl. When I went to Chaussy it was like stepping back in time. Most people don't even have cars or running water."

"Who decides which children come here?" Mr. Nelson asked.

"A group of women in Chaussy selects the neediest children between eight and twelve years old."

"Who pays the children's airfare?" Mrs. Nelson said.

"Transportation is arranged by the fund in Ottawa, but the sponsoring families pay the child's airfare and all their expenses in Canada."

Sharon asked who would stay with the children during the day. Mrs. Nelson explained that she'd be at home all summer because she hadn't been able to get a mediation job.

"That's interesting, Lyn. I'm a lawyer myself. We have people specializing in mediation in our office," Sharon said.

"I love my work," Mrs. Nelson said, "but a summer at home doing things with the kids will be fun too."

"Hosting a child from Belarus can be a challenge, but you seem like the kind of family who could take it on," Sharon said. "You'll be hearing from the committee."

When Mr. and Mrs. Nelson walked Sharon out to her car Gram and Jillian went back to playing rummy. Gram dealt another hand.

"Sounds like quite an adjustment for a little girl," Gram said, her brown eyes and round face concerned.

"Oh, no," Jillian said. "She'll be fine. I'm going to save my allowance to buy her something special. Besides, I'll be with her every minute, you know, to show her around. She'll love it here."

"Quite a lot of responsibility for you."

"I'm up to it."

"Gin," said Gram, laughing. "That's three games for me, eight for you. Here's fifty cents."

"A good start for our Belarus fund," Jillian said.

For three whole weeks Jillian kept her wish a secret. She hadn't told one person at school, not Ms. Kaminsky, not Ross.

Today 6B was going on a field trip to Science World. No one wanted to partner with Jillian, so she had to pair up with Ms. Kaminsky. When they got to the electrostatic ball, kids took turns touching it, then laughing like crazy when their hair stood on end. Jillian walked ahead to the dinosaur exhibit. The field trip seemed to go on forever.

When the bus dropped everyone back at school, Jillian's mother greeted her with a hug and they walked home together.

"You look down in the dumps, Jillian. Why don't

you check the mail when you get home? There might be something to cheer you up."

On the hall table was a letter from the selection committee. Jillian tore it open and read out loud: "We are pleased to confirm your sponsorship of Tanya Velikaya. She will arrive in Canada on June 26 and return to Belarus August 31."

The letter went on to say that Tanya was eleven and lived with her parents, her fourteen-year-old sister Mariana and her grandmother.

Jillian grinned. "She's the same age as me, Mom! And she arrives on June 26 — one day before school ends! Can you believe it?" Jillian whirled in a circle, waving the letter. "I'm taking her to school the first day she gets here!"

I'd like you to meet my friend, Tanya.

Jillian read the letter twice more to herself and then she read it to David, who insisted she slow down.

When her father came home she tried to keep her excitement under control, reading it to him as slowly as she could.

"Great news!" Dad said. "Now we're committed to contributing one thousand dollars for Tanya's airfare."

"No price is too high for friendship," Jillian said.

Her father glared at Jillian, who suddenly realized what she'd said. "Just kidding," she mumbled.

"I wondered there for a minute."

"I'll help to earn the money. Mr. Woodman's hurt his knee and needs someone to walk Tessie every afternoon. I'll go next door and see him right now."

Tessie was a small white poodle with bright black eyes, floppy ears and a perky tail that switched back and forth like a windshield wiper.

Mr. Woodman handed Jillian two plastic bags. "I'm sure you know what these are for," he said with a grin.

"Yep, I know," Jillian sighed, desperately hoping the bags wouldn't be needed.

Tessie pranced along the sidewalk, digging her nose under every rock and around every post and turning her head every two minutes to see if Jillian was paying attention. When she headed for the bushes, Jillian's heart sank.

Jillian's pickup was not always tidy, but by the end of the second week, both her technique and Mr. Woodman's knee had improved.

"I got paid twenty-five dollars," Jillian called from the steps as her dad came back from the office.

"Great work," he answered. "You must be pleased."

"I'm pleased I have a cat," Jillian said.

★

Another month of school dragged by, but they were definitely making progress on the Belarus project. In May, Jillian's parents went to a meeting with the other host parents. They reported to Jillian and David the next morning.

"There are thirty-two groups like ours in Canada. Our group has six families, all of them from the

Vancouver area, including some who live out in the valley," Mr. Nelson said. "We've arranged to get the families together for a picnic in the middle of the summer."

Mrs. Nelson added, "Sharon told us to be sure the children have plenty of rest when they first arrive. She also said dental care in Belarus is poor and suggested we make appointments for them with our dentists. Apparently there's no problem getting the kids to eat. They're used to a diet of potatoes and cabbage, but they'll probably like all our food."

That morning, Mrs. Nelson mailed the cheque for the airfare, which included the money Jillian made walking Tessie and playing rummy with Gram. They taped a map of the world on the fridge door with a line drawn from Minsk, the capital of Belarus, halfway around the world to Vancouver. Jillian looked at the map every morning, then at the calendar, counting down the days to Tanya's arrival.

Upstairs, Tanya's room was ready. On the bed was a yellow-flowered quilt and on the wall Jillian and her mother had hung a poster of a ballerina. Jillian cut stars as big as her hand out of silver paper and climbed on top of the dresser to tape them to the ceiling. Then she lay back on the soft quilt and looked up, wishing with all her heart for June 26 to come quickly.

THREE

It was past ten o'clock, dark but still warm, on the night of June 26 and the Nelsons were waiting in the airport lounge. Jillian squirmed in the hard metal chair and twisted her fingers through the thick, amber-coloured fur of a stuffed bear, her welcome gift for Tanya.

Mr. and Mrs. Nelson had said hello to one family they recognized from the orientation meeting, but most of the other families were scattered around the large lounge.

"Those poor kids," Mrs. Nelson said. "It's a fourteen-hour plane trip. They go from Minsk to Moscow to London, then to Toronto and Vancouver. And they're coming to stay with people they don't even know."

"I'd be scared," Jillian said.

"Me too, knowing our family," David said, laughing and stretching his long legs.

David always teased when he was excited. His hair gel was pretty thick tonight too.

Suddenly, Jillian reached for her father's arm. "I can't catch anything from Tanya can I?"

"No, of course not," he said. "Exposure to radiation isn't contagious."

"Yeah, but exposure to our family could be serious," David said.

"I'm too tired to even laugh at that," Jillian said.

The glare from the overhead lights in the lounge made Jillian want to close her eyes and her stomach felt funny. It had been like this all day.

"The screen says the plane's due in fifteen minutes," Mrs. Nelson said.

Jillian clutched the bear tightly and reviewed her plan. She and Tanya would get to know each other in the car and when they got home she'd take Tanya to her new bedroom and help her unpack. She pictured herself turning down the quilt and giving the tired girl a cup of cocoa, then telling her about school the next day, Jillian's last day in 6B.

I'd like you to meet my friend, Tanya.

The Nelsons joined the other families gathered near the gate. A loud voice crackled from a speaker announcing the plane's arrival and a few minutes later a small cluster of children, sticking close to each other, were guided through the gate by a stewardess. Jillian counted five girls and one small boy, each one pale and serious.

Sharon Skene went forward, thanked the stewardess and gave each child a welcoming hug before talking to the group in Russian. Then she turned to the waiting families.

"These children are happy to be in Canada, but it's been a long trip and they're tired. Let's get them into bed as soon as we can. When I call each child's name, will the sponsoring family please come forward?"

"Sasha," Sharon said. A woman and a tall girl about David's age came out of the crowd; each put an arm around the small boy. One of the girls from Belarus bent to kiss Sasha goodbye before his new family took him quickly out the airport doors.

"Nina."

A dark-skinned man in a white turban stepped forward to greet the girl who'd just said goodbye to Sasha.

"We heard a brother and sister were coming. Luckily their hosting families live close to each other," Mrs. Nelson said as she watched Nina and the man in the turban carrying her small suitcase head for the parking lot.

Sharon called "Yulia," "Anya," "Olga," and, one by one, families came forward to greet the children.

Desperately, Jillian looked around the room. Why didn't Sharon call Tanya's name? Maybe something had happened and Tanya wasn't coming! Then Jillian saw a thin girl with an old black suitcase standing behind Sharon.

"There's someone by herself," Jillian said, pointing to the girl with tangled brown hair hanging in front of her face. "Maybe that's Tanya."

Even as she said the words, Jillian found herself

hoping it wasn't true. The girl was too scrawny and sad looking.

Finally Sharon called, "Tanya," and sure enough, Tanya was the girl with the black suitcase.

The Nelsons reached her quickly; Jillian could see Tanya had been crying. She wore a grey jacket with sleeves that were too short and a faded black skirt that just covered her knees. Her legs were bare and her brown canvas shoes had holes in them.

Jillian's mother put her arms around Tanya's shoulders and smoothed back her hair. "We're so glad you've come, Tanya."

Her father leaned forward to give Tanya his handkerchief. He signalled to Jillian to come closer. "Tanya, this is our daughter Jillian."

Tanya sniffled and darted a look at Jillian, who shyly handed Tanya the amber bear. "It's for you."

Without nodding or smiling, Tanya took the bear and tucked it tightly under one arm.

David shuffled forward awkwardly and his voice cracked as he said, "Welcome to Canada, Tanya. I'm David. I'll carry your suitcase."

As they walked to the parking lot, Jillian saw that the night sky had filled with stars. While she waited for her father to unlock the car, Jillian tried to get a better look at Tanya. Behind the stringy hair, she saw a wide face with green eyes, the lids heavy with exhaustion. Tanya's mouth was tight and her pale cheeks were marked with several scabby sores.

On the way home, Tanya sat silently between David

and Jillian, her head down. Jillian touched Tanya's arm to get her attention.

"Tired, Tanya?" Jillian tried a hand signal: she pressed her palms together, placed her head on them and closed her eyes. "Want to sleep?"

No response.

"Remember, Tanya can't understand English," her father said. "Just smile at her. That's all she wants tonight."

Jillian smiled. Tanya didn't. David shrugged his shoulders.

Once inside the house, Mrs. Nelson took Tanya upstairs to her bedroom, calling, "It's late, Jillian. Come and say good night when you're ready for bed."

Jillian brushed her teeth in a rush and dashed upstairs to get Tanya's bed ready, but her mother had already pulled down the covers and Tanya stood by the wall with her back turned. She was sliding her feet out of those awful shoes.

"Like me to help?" Jillian said. Tanya didn't turn around.

"The best way to help now is to say good night," her mother said.

"But Mom, I have to get to know her," Jillian pleaded.

"Tomorrow, Jillian. Say good night now."

"Night, Tanya."

There was no answer. *Did this girl talk?*

Jillian picked up Chester and was sliding under the quilt as her mother came into the room.

"That poor girl's so thin I can feel her shoulder blades. And there are no clothes in her suitcase. I have to borrow one of your nightgowns."

Great! A girl with stringy hair who doesn't smile or even look at you! And she had ugly sores on her face! The long summer stretched ahead, weeks and weeks with *that* girl.

As Jillian drifted off to sleep, she saw herself standing by Ms. Kaminsky's desk, her arm around Tanya's shoulders, everyone in the class looking up admiringly at her. They were looking up at Jillian, the girl they had ignored, the fine person who was devoting her entire summer to the care of an unfortunate girl. They were clapping.

One second after Jillian's eyes opened, she remembered that Tanya was in the next room. She jumped out of bed and dressed quickly. As she buttoned her favourite sweater, her dad called, "Breakfast, Jillian!"

She rushed to Tanya's room, but saw it was empty. She dashed downstairs and found Tanya sitting with David and her parents around the kitchen table. Tanya's head was down and her hands were folded in her lap. The bowl of cereal in front of her hadn't been touched.

Jillian sat down next to Tanya, leaned over and spoke slowly, "How-are-you-this-morning, Tanya?"

No answer. No smile. Her long hair was uncombed and the spots on her face were even redder than they'd been the night before. Jillian tried not to stare at the worn jacket, the thin skirt and those horrible shoes. How to get her attention? Jillian got up and stood beside the fridge.

"Look, Tanya." Jillian moved her finger across the map. "Here's Belarus and here's Vancouver, all the way over on this side of the world." She flashed an enthusiastic smile. "Your new home!"

Tanya glanced quickly toward the map, then back down at her hands.

Jillian tried again. "You know what? You're coming to school with me today!" Jillian smiled eagerly and nodded her head up and down like a yo-yo. "School … books … teacher!" She waited. "Okay?"

No answer.

"The kid's sure quiet," David said.

Jillian looked at her mother and raised her eyebrows.

"Tanya's shy and she's tired," Mrs. Nelson said. "We'll have to be patient." She reached over and placed her hand on Tanya's arm.

Tanya lifted her head and smiled weakly at Mrs. Nelson. Jillian saw brown stains on the girl's teeth. *Gross*. She looked at David, who was smiling at Tanya. If he'd noticed the stains, he didn't show it.

After a minute, Tanya picked up a spoon and started eating.

"Like it?" Jillian asked, catching Tanya's eye and pointing to the cereal.

Tanya nodded.

"I'm Jillian," she said slowly and clearly, her finger pointing to her own face. "JILLIAN."

"Jil-l-ian," Tanya said in a soft voice.

"Very good," Jillian said, even more pleased with herself. "Tanya, I know two Russian words. *Privét* means 'hello' and *da svidániya* means 'goodbye'."

Tanya smiled. "*Privét*, Jil-l-ian. Toilet."

The Nelsons looked at her.

"No," said Tanya.

Mr. Nelson said, "'Toilet' and 'no'. Two excellent words for a young girl so far from home."

"Finally! She's talking!" Jillian said.

"Here's some jam for your toast, Tanya," Mrs. Nelson said.

Tanya took the jar, dug in her knife and began to spread it on her toast.

"We say 'thank you,' Tanya," said Jillian's mother.

"*Spasíba*. Tha-ank you," Tanya said, her mouth full.

"You are welcome," said Jillian's mother.

"You-are-welcome," Tanya said proudly.

"We-are-making-progress-here," Jillian said, and, this time, Tanya laughed with them.

Mr. Nelson went to his desk and came back with two small red pocket dictionaries.

"We'll need these," he said, handing one to Tanya and one to Jillian. "Tanya has her own copy and we'll share the other."

He demonstrated to Tanya by opening up the dictionary. "You look up the Russian word in the front half of the dictionary and there beside it is the English word."

Tanya nodded and flipped through several pages.

"What should *I* do?" Jillian asked.

"You look up the English word in the second half of the dictionary and find the Russian word beside it."

"Good. I'll take it to school with us today," Jillian said.

"Sorry, Jillian," her mother said. "I can see Tanya's far too tired."

"What? Come on!" Jillian felt panicky. "She'll be fine. There are kids I want her to meet."

"Tanya needs to sleep."

"She can sleep anytime! Let her come with me, just for the morning," Jillian pleaded. "I promise to bring her home at lunchtime. I just want to show her ... introduce her to the kids."

"Can't you see she can hardly keep her eyes open?" her father said. "In Belarus, people are just going to bed now. She's got a bad case of jet lag."

Jillian pushed the chair back and stood up. "Just how long does this 'lag' last, anyway?"

"Maybe a few days. But don't worry. She'll soon adjust to our time zone," her father said.

"*Soon*? I need to take her to school *today*. I've been planning this for months." Jillian picked up her cereal bowl and slammed it in the sink.

"I know you're disappointed, but you need to think of Tanya. Now off you go," her mother said.

"I *am* thinking of Tanya. It's important for her to see a Canadian school," Jillian yelled.

"No, Jillian. I'm taking Tanya to her bedroom now. Say goodbye."

Jillian glared at her parents and shot a look at the stranger who slouched in the kitchen chair. She grabbed her lunch bag. Maybe it wasn't so bad. Tanya didn't look that great.

"*Da svidániya*, Tanya," Jillian said crossly. She stomped down the front stairs on the way to her very last day in 6B.

FOUR

Tanya and Mrs. Nelson were waiting at the door when Jillian came up the front steps after school. Tanya was wearing a blouse with a green-trimmed collar and a pair of green shorts. She was smiling. "Allo, Jil-l-ian."

"Hi, Tanya," Jillian said.

"How was your last day?" said Jillian's mother.

"All the girls had autograph books and got their friends to sign them. I didn't want to write in their stupid books anyway!" Jillian grabbed a cookie from the tray. "Ms. Kaminsky wished me good luck in grade seven. I'll need it."

"Grade seven is a long way off. Things could look very different in two months," her mother said.

Sitting on the front steps, munching cookies and drinking raspberry juice, Jillian tried to figure out a way to talk to Tanya.

She touched Tanya's blouse. "I like your new …"

Mrs. Nelson handed Jillian the dictionary. "Never go anywhere without our little red book."

Jillian flipped to B … blouse … *Blúzka*.

"Nice *blúzka*," she said to Tanya.

"Nice *blúzka*," Tanya repeated.

"Blouse," said Jillian.

"Blo-ouse," said Tanya.

Jillian could see it would be one word at a time.

Lyn Nelson sat on the step beside the girls and rolled up the sleeves of her T-shirt to sun her arms. "Tanya slept all morning, then I took her to the mall. She was almost too scared to get on the escalator, but she loved the display of beach balls and sun umbrellas. You know the big fountain? They had mannequins in bathing suits around it. I could hardly get her to leave so we could have a hamburger."

"You had lunch at the mall?" Jillian's throat felt tight. "What else did you buy?"

"We got the clothes she's wearing, a toothbrush, a pair of jeans, some T-shirts, underwear, a pair of pyjamas and white running shoes. She likes everything except the shoes."

"The blouse is really nice. Why didn't you buy one for me?"

"You don't *need* any more summer clothes, Jillian."

"I don't get it. If Tanya was okay to go shopping, why wasn't she okay to come to school with me?"

"I told you. She had a rest before we went shopping.

There's no rush. You're going to have lots of time with Tanya."

Before Jillian could figure out how she felt about that, Chester padded around the corner from the backyard and Jillian picked him up.

"Tanya, from Belarus, I'd like you to meet Chester, from Vancouver."

Tanya took Chester in her arms and held him tightly, her cheek against his face.

"Tanya's already met Chester," Mrs. Nelson said. "She loves cats."

Tanya was talking to the cat in strange Russian words. "*Kótik, kótik*," she said quietly.

Jillian stood up. "Enough, Tanya!" She made a rough grab for Chester, who arched his back and wiggled free, bounding down the steps and around the side of the house.

"Maybe this is a good time to show Tanya the things in your bedroom, Jillian," her mother suggested.

Upstairs, Tanya's eyes grew wider and wider at each new treasure. She tried on all the beaded necklaces in the dresser drawer. She picked up and scattered the CDs from the shelf. She spread Jillian's magazines on the floor and flipped through them roughly. It was like having Tessie wiggling and sniffing all over her bedroom.

Tanya went to the closet and came out with Jillian's new black party shoes. She had a pleading look in her eyes. "*Pazhálusta*."

Apparently *pazhálusta* meant "please." "Okay, try them on," Jillian nodded.

"*Krasívaya túfli!*" Tanya said, smiling as she looked down at the shiny shoes, turning her foot to admire the square heel.

Jillian found *krasívaya* in the dictionary. Beautiful. Next she found *túfli*. Shoes. Yes, her shoes *were* beautiful with a strap across the top and half-inch heels. Jillian had worn them only once, at her father's birthday party.

She watched apprehensively as Tanya pranced across the room and stopped to examine the items on the dresser.

"Don't touch my music box, *pazhálusta*," Jillian said. She pointed to the window seat. "Sit. I'll show you."

The girls sat on the window seat and Jillian wound the key. The lid opened, the platform swung up and the music began. The tiny fairy, holding the shining star in the air, twirled to the music.

> *When you wish upon a star,*
> *Makes no difference who you are,*
> *Anything your heart desires*
> *will come to you.*

"Oh-h-h," Tanya said softly and Jillian saw the look of wonder in her green eyes.

"This music box is the most *krasívaya* thing I own. Tanya. It's very, very special," Jillian said sternly. She pointed to the key and shook her head. "No. *Nyet*. Never wind the key yourself."

Tanya nodded and gestured to Jillian. Even without

words, Jillian understood how much Tanya wanted to hear the music one more time so she wound the key again.

The song played itself through again and their eyes met.

"*Spasíba*. Thank you, Jill-i-an," Tanya said, her mouth curling into a wide smile.

Oh, no, those stained teeth.

When the girls came down for dinner, Tanya was still wearing the black shoes.

"Kind of you to let Tanya wear your new shoes," her mom said, putting a hand on Jillian's shoulder.

"I let her try them on and now she doesn't want to take them off," Jillian whispered.

Tanya ate all the food on her plate: ham, potatoes, carrots and salad. Then she ate two apples and two bananas.

"She likes our food!" Jillian exclaimed.

"Drink your milk, please, Tanya," Mrs. Nelson said, holding Tanya's glass.

"*Nyet.*" Tanya made a sour face and turned her head away.

"She's probably just tired," Jillian's mother said.

"Just be careful you don't spoil her," Jillian warned.

"Why not read to Tanya tonight?" Jillian's dad suggested. "Pick some books you liked when you were younger.

Poetry is an excellent way to teach someone to read."

Jillian sat on Tanya's bed and read first from *The Cat in the Hat* with its easy rhymes and then the poem "The Owl and the Pussycat."

> *The Owl and the Pussycat went to sea*
> *In a beautiful pea-green boat,*
> *They took some honey, and plenty of money,*
> *Wrapped up in a five-pound note.*

Tanya repeated the verse very seriously, even though she didn't have any idea what the words meant.

She looked around the room. "*Bolshóy dom,* Jillian."

Jillian grabbed the red dictionary.

"Big house? You think our house is big? I've never thought about that. Guess it's bigger than your apartment."

Tanya snuggled under the covers and Jillian left the room, keeping the door partly open in case Tanya called out in the night.

Later, in bed, she heard sounds coming from Tanya's room. She got up and listened at the door.

"Jill-i-an, Da-vid, Ches-ter. Jill-i-an, Da-vid. Ches-ter."

Tanya said the names over and over and Jillian's name was always first.

★

At breakfast the next morning the girls kept sneaking looks at each other. When Jillian slurped her juice,

Tanya slurped hers louder. Jillian crossed her eyes; Tanya made her eyes roll back in her head. Tanya burped loudly and Jillian burped too. Then Tanya put a piece of toast on the top of her head, jam side down. Giggling, Jillian thought that for a kid without words, Tanya could be a lot of fun.

"Tanya's not the shy, well-mannered girl I'd imagined," Mrs. Nelson said. "In fact, she's a Belarusian version of you, Jillian Nelson."

David was thinking the same thing. That night Jillian heard him telling Gram on the phone, "Tanya's exactly like my sister except she doesn't talk as much, which is a big relief."

It was Saturday morning and David was dressed in his baseball uniform for his eleven o'clock game. Tanya was wearing her new clothes, but had kept on her old brown canvas shoes.

They found seats in the bleachers and Tanya didn't take her eyes off David. When he hit a long ball to right field, Jillian and her parents stood and yelled, "Go, David! Go!"

David made it to first base, then second and by the time he reached third, Tanya was on her feet, too.

"Go-David-go. Yea-ah, Nel-son!" she yelled along with the others.

"She's a quick learner," commented Mrs. Nelson.

Between innings Jillian's dad bought them hot dogs piled with mustard, relish and ketchup.

Jillian watched anxiously as Tanya took her first bite. "You like it? Is it good?"

No answer, just chewing.

"Good?" Mr. Nelson asked.

"You-are-welcome," answered the girl proudly, ketchup running down her chin. The Nelsons laughed so hard that everyone in the bleachers turned to look at them.

At home, Mrs. Nelson served raspberries and blue-berries for dessert.

"Good *frúkty*," said Tanya.

"Yes, the fruit is good," said Jillian. "Hey, what do you know? I can understand Russian!"

Jillian's mother poured three glasses of milk, but Tanya pushed her milk away. "*Nyet malakó!*"

"But Tanya, milk is good too!" Jillian said.

David bent both arms and flexed his biceps. "Gives you muscles!"

"*Nyet*," Tanya said, taking her milk to the sink and dumping it. She sat back down, scowling.

Jillian's mom took a deep breath and her dad frowned, but David continued eating.

"Something's bothering her," Jillian said.

"Isn't the soil in Belarus contaminated with radia-tion?" David asked.

"Yes, that's what Ms. Kaminsky told us."

"Well, if the soil's contaminated, then so is the grass that grows in the soil. Cows eat the grass."

"Their milk is contaminated!" Jillian exclaimed.

"We can't force the girl to drink something that scares her," David said.

"No problem. We'll have ice cream with all our meals!" said Jillian.

"How about yoghurt and cheese?" suggested her father.

Jillian looked up from the dictionary. "You mean *yógurt* and *syr*."

That night Sharon came for a visit. Tanya sat beside her on the couch and they talked rapidly in Russian.

Sharon said, "Tanya tells me she likes having her own bedroom. In Chaussy, she and her sister Mariana have to share a bedroom with their *bábushka*."

"Three people in one bedroom?" Jillian asked.

"Yes. Her *máma* and *pápa* sleep on a pullout couch in the living room. And their bathroom is shared with four other families on the same floor," Sharon said. "They're lucky to have hot water."

"Our family has trouble sharing *one* bathroom," Jillian said.

Tanya whispered to Sharon and led her upstairs. They came down a few moments later with presents from Tanya's suitcase for the family: a bottle of vodka, an embroidered tablecloth and some candy.

"*Spasíba*, Tanya," said the Nelsons.

Tanya's parents had sent a note that Sharon translated.

*We thank your family for having Tanya to visit you
in Canada. We have great hope in you.*
From Igor and Galina Velikaya

"It's an act of faith, allowing Tanya to stay with us,"
Mrs. Nelson said, shaking her head.

Shyly, Tanya passed around a photograph of her
family seated at a table set with dishes, a cake and a
bottle of vodka. Behind them, electrical wires ran up
the wall beside a large needlework picture.

"*Den razhdéniya bábushka,*" Tanya said proudly.

"The photo was taken at her grandmother's birthday last year," Sharon translated.

Tanya's *bábushka* looked older than Gram. She had
grey hair and green eyes and she wore a white lace
blouse and black skirt. Tanya's father had his arm
around his wife, who was wearing a dark flowered dress.
Mariana and Tanya stood together. Both had long hair,
but while Tanya had her grandmother's full face,
Mariana's was pale and thin. Tanya was making a *v* with
two fingers behind her sister's head and Mariana was
returning the favour.

"Tanya's *pápa* is an electrician and her *máma* works
as a seamstress in a factory. Her *pápa* plays the accor-
dion and the family likes to sing along."

Tanya said something else to Sharon, who translated, "Tanya's a little homesick, so I've suggested she
write to them."

"Hope she tells them she likes us," Jillian said
uncertainly.

"She will," Sharon said. "And now, Tanya wants to show you something she can do."

Tanya took a circle of red string from her pocket and wrapped it around the backs of both hands. She twisted her fingers, smoothly and quickly looping the string once. Then she dipped the middle finger of each hand to hook the opposite strings, pulled her hands apart and held them proudly in the air.

"*Kravát kot!*" she announced, turning her hands so everyone could have a look.

"I know! We call it Cat's Cradle!" Jillian said. "It's hard to do."

Again Tanya flipped her fingers, hooked and pulled the string over her thumbs three times and held up another creation.

"Cat's whiskers!" translated Sharon after Tanya explained.

The long spiky strings held taut between Tanya's hands looked just like Chester's whiskers.

"Wish I knew how to do that," Jillian said.

FIVE

"Busy day, girls," Jillian's mother said. "You both have appointments with the dentist, then Tanya gets her hair cut and in the afternoon Gram's coming over."

"*Mashína, mashína!*" Tanya yelled, running down the steps and taking over the passenger seat of the car.

"She acts like she *owns* our car," Jillian said from the back seat.

"I'm sure she hardly ever gets to ride in a car," her mother said sharply. "Let her enjoy the front seat."

"Guess that means I'll be riding in the back all summer."

"You'll *both* be riding in the back seat as soon as I pick up Sharon. She's coming with us to translate."

In the elevator up to the dentist's office, Sharon and Tanya chattered back and forth in Russian. Jillian tugged at her mother's sleeve. "Mom, people are staring at them."

"Rude, isn't it?" her mother said.

In the waiting room, Jillian looked up from a magazine and noticed Tanya twisting her hands in her lap.

"Don't be scared," Jillian smiled reassuringly. "Dr. Bridge is very gentle. I'll go first."

When Jillian returned to the waiting room, she waved a new toothbrush. "No cavities! But guess what? Dr. Bridge says I might need braces in the fall. Railway tracks like Molly!"

"Is Molly a friend from school?" Mrs. Nelson said.

"Not really," Jillian answered, picking up a magazine.

Half an hour later Dr. Bridge came out with Sharon and Tanya, who was clutching a new toothbrush as well.

"What a brave girl! Tanya has four big cavities," Dr. Bridge said. "When you come back to get them filled I'll polish those front teeth and get rid of the stains. See you soon."

Mrs. Nelson dropped Sharon at the library and then drove to Susan's Hair Design. The salon was brightly lit with a row of chairs facing a wall of mirrors. Tanya wrinkled her nose at the smell of hairsprays and chemicals.

A woman with a wide smile and short dark hair led Tanya to the washbasins and swooshed a green nylon cape over her shoulders.

"It's lovely hair," Susan said, "but too long and thick to manage. Let's cut it, just to here," she said, putting her hand a little above Tanya's shoulders.

When Tanya's hair had been cut and dried, she tossed her head breezily from side to side and grinned at her reflection. "*Dóbra. Dóbra.* Good. I like," she said as Susan held up a hand mirror so Tanya could see the back.

"With those bangs trimmed, you can really see her beautiful green eyes," Jillian's mother said.

Jillian looked at her own reflection in the bright mirror. Her eyes were ordinary blue. Her hair was plain brown and limp.

Halfway home, she made a decision. "I'll be growing my hair long this summer, Mom. And, by the way, people had better watch it. Tanya is getting vain from all these compliments."

Her mother gave her a silencing look in the rear-view mirror.

When they arrived home, Mrs. Nelson said, "I want to capture this summer on film. Wait here while I get my camera."

She had the girls stand side by side on the front lawn. They both wore jean skirts and were exactly the same height.

"Say cheese," said Mrs. Nelson.

Tanya kept her mouth closed. Jillian couldn't manage even a weak smile.

"Gram's here!" Jillian yelled as she ran down the front steps after lunch.

"How's it going?" Gram asked, getting out of the car

and giving Jillian a big hug.

"It's okay," Jillian answered. She was about to ask if they could play rummy when Gram spotted David and Tanya.

"Hi, David. And this must be Tanya." She shook Tanya's hand.

Tanya looked at the ground. Jillian looked disgusted.

"She's only pretending to be shy, Gram."

"I can understand a bit of shyness," said Gram, looking from one girl to the other. "Don't the two of you look alike!"

Jillian raised her eyebrows and peered across at Tanya, who was leaning on the handlebars of David's bike.

"Tanya wants to learn to ride," David said.

"Why don't I teach her?" Gram said. "We can get to know each other. Can we use your bike, Jillian?"

Jillian bit her lip. "I guess."

Jillian went to the swing and pushed herself with one foot, watching Gram and Tanya in the driveway. It wasn't long before Tanya could ride well enough to balance all the way by herself.

"Jillian, how do I say 'good work'?" Gram called.

"*Dóbra*," Jillian answered.

"Very *dóbra*, Tanya." Gram smiled and gave Tanya a hug.

"Okay, *Bábushka*."

"Gram! Gram! Come and push me!" Jillian yelled.

Gram pushed her on the swing for a while and then they sat in a shady spot on the grass.

"Why so glum, Jillian? Things not working out between you and Tanya?" Gram asked.

"Not really. I feel sorry for her because of where she comes from and everything, but she always has to get her own way. She acts like she owns the place and plays with all my things."

"It's good to learn how to share."

"I already know how to share. I have to share with my stupid brother all the time."

After they all had tea in the backyard, Jillian overheard her mother and Gram talking in the kitchen.

"How's it going?" Gram asked.

"Tanya's quite a girl — has a mind of her own, just like our Jillian. They got on well initially, but now Tanya's getting lots of attention and I'm afraid Jillian's nose is out of joint."

"She's used to being the only girl in the house," Gram said.

Jillian's eavesdropping was interrupted as David and Tanya came down the hall.

"Let's go! I'll take you both on at badminton," David said.

"You're on," said Jillian, running to get the racquets.

"You-rr-on," repeated Tanya, running after her.

David set up a net in the backyard and right from the start it was clear that Tanya was a good player. It was also clear that Jillian wasn't. In fact, Jillian could barely get the badminton bird over the net.

When Gram came to tell them she was off to her Spanish lesson, Tanya and David went over to say good-bye, but Jillian kept her head in the bushes, searching for a lost bird.

"Let's get on with the game," David called, shifting his feet from side to side across the net from the girls.

"Way to go!" he said when Tanya returned a difficult shot.

"Here's one for you, Jillian," said David, lobbing an easy serve to his sister. Jillian swung at the bird and missed it by a mile.

"You have to run for it!" he called.

"I'm trying as hard as I can, David! Quit being so mean to me!" Jillian threw down the racquet and ran into the house.

"What's the matter?" said her mother, looking up from where she lay reading on the couch.

"It's David. He ignores me and sends all the good shots to Tanya. Then he yells at me."

"Please stop whining, Jillian."

"Everyone's nicer to Tanya than they are to me."

"Tanya's our guest. Of course we're nice to her and of course people show her attention and give her compliments. Is it just possible you're jealous?"

"Hi, Jill-i-an," said Tanya, coming into the bedroom. Jillian sat on her window seat with a book in front of her, but she was not reading; she was thinking dark thoughts.

"*Múzyka?*" Tanya asked, looking at the music box.

"*Nyet! Nyet!*" Jillian said loudly. "Don't touch the music box!" She pointed to the closet. "You can play with my Barbies in the box."

Jillian watched out of the corner of her eye as Tanya disappeared into the closet and came out with the black party shoes.

"*Nyet.* You can't wear my shoes," said Jillian, shaking her head firmly.

Tanya looked straight at Jillian, then let the shoes drop and walked out of the room.

A few minutes later Jillian found her mother and Tanya sitting downstairs on the couch. Mrs. Nelson had her arm around Tanya.

"Poor thing, she looks so sad. She's such a long way from home," Jillian's mother said.

"She's *not* homesick. She's just mad because I won't let her wear my shoes or play with my music box."

"Really? And why won't you?"

"Because I don't want my stuff wrecked."

"You are lucky to *have* so many things, Jillian. Can't you share?"

"I shared all my Barbies with her! She can play with them any time she wants."

"What's up with you, Jillian? One day you let Tanya wear your shoes and the next day you won't. Today you won't let her play with anything but the old Barbies that *you* don't even play with any more. She must be as confused as I am and probably wishes she could go home and leave us all behind."

Tanya looked from Mrs. Nelson to Jillian, then buried her face in a cushion.

Jillian's mother shook her head. "I'm really upset, Jillian. I think I've spoiled you. Maybe because you're the youngest child and the only girl in the family you haven't yet learned you're not the centre of the universe."

At supper, both girls were cranky. Tanya ate too much fruit and scowled when Mr. Nelson took the bowl of cherries away.

"She's a fruit freak," Jillian said sharply.

"You're the freak," said David.

"Thanks a lot," Jillian said, tears springing to her eyes. "Why does everyone take her side?"

"I'm going crazy surrounded by little girls," David said. "I should be spending time with girls my own age."

"Before you go out looking, remember tomorrow's our Canada Day potluck dinner," said Mr. Nelson. "We've invited the neighbours, just like we did in Ottawa."

"This year's special because we're welcoming Tanya to Canada," Mrs. Nelson added.

"So how am I supposed to explain Canada Day to Tanya?" Jillian snapped.

"Look it up," her mother replied, handing Jillian the red dictionary.

Jillian hurled the book on the table. "I'm sick of looking things up in the stupid dictionary. It takes too long and it's too much like school."

David grabbed the dictionary. "Here's how to say Canada's birthday: *Den razhdéniya Kanáda.*"

Jillian groaned.

"Say *razh-den-iya*," David said patiently.

"The stupid words are too hard," said Jillian.

"Calm down, Jillian. Sound it out," her dad said.

"No. I don't want to speak Russian. And no one can make me!"

Jillian gave Tanya a long black look, but Tanya's eyes were downcast and she missed it.

"Time for bed," Mrs. Nelson said.

"NO BED!" said Tanya.

"Heaven help us," Mr. Nelson moaned. "Girls this age must be the same all over the world."

Upstairs, Jillian's mother put cream on Tanya's cheeks. "Time to brush your teeth," she said.

"NO!" Tanya answered grumpily.

Mrs. Nelson rolled her eyes and sighed.

"'No' is the first word Tanya learned. Can't blame her for using it," David said coming up the stairs.

"Jillian, please go and brush your teeth with Tanya," her mother said.

"I'm too tired. Let her skip a night."

"Someone needs an attitude adjustment," David said.

"You think Tanya's so perfect, David Nelson. You go and spit in the sink with her!"

SIX

Jillian looked out the dining-room window to where Tanya sat on the grass in the afternoon sun. Tanya wore a sleeveless shirt and overalls and still, probably stuck to her feet by now, those old canvas shoes. Her arms were wrapped around Chester. Jillian walked over to her and heard Tanya singing in Russian. She looked lonely, staring into the trees.

"*Krasívaya*," Jillian said. "Beautiful."

"Belarus," Tanya said.

"I like it," Jillian said, sitting down beside her.

"I sing about *serébryaniye beryózy i azyóra* in Belarus."

"Can you tell me in English?" Jillian handed the dictionary to Tanya.

"Belarus. Land of silver birch trees and lakes," the homesick girl said. "*Krasívaya*."

The song could be about Canada, Jillian thought.

★

"Come and help me unload the car," Gram called. "I've got all the fixings for do-it-yourself sundaes."

Mr. and Mrs. Leyland from across the street arrived carrying a green salad. Mr. Woodman walked up the driveway balancing a tray of crackers and cheese. Sharon came in carrying an enormous watermelon. Mrs. Nelson looked relieved to see her.

"Could you stay after the party, Sharon?" she asked. "I need to talk."

"Sure," Sharon said. "Now let me give you a hand."

The neighbours clustered around Tanya. "How do you do? *Privét*, Tanya," they said.

Tanya acted shy and held onto Mrs. Nelson's sleeve, covering her mouth with her hand.

Everyone had brought her gifts: a purse with three loonies from Gram, a book about Canada from Mr. Woodman and a large bag of coloured jewellery beads from the Leylands.

Jillian pulled on her mother's sleeve. "It's not fair," she said. "No one, not even Gram, brought a present for *me*. Everything is for Tanya."

"They know you've got more toys and games than Tanya will ever have."

"Everybody likes her better."

"That's not true, Jillian. Just because people like Tanya doesn't mean they don't like you." Her mother turned and walked into the kitchen to get the food ready.

Jillian stood digging the toe of her running shoe into

the grass until her father called. "Come on, Jillian. Help David get the badminton games organized."

After the tournament, the hot dogs, the burgers, the do-it-yourself sundaes and the watermelon, Jillian and David passed around small Canadian flags.

Mr. Nelson said, "Everyone gather in a circle. We're going to sing 'O Canada!'"

This was the part Jillian had always liked best when they'd lived in Ottawa.

O Canada! Our home and native land!

At first they all felt embarrassed singing in a garden, but her dad's strong voice got them going.

With glowing hearts we see thee rise,
The True North strong and free!

Across the lawn Jillian saw Tanya standing by David and looking up at him as he sang. What did Tanya know about Canada anyway?

As the Leylands were leaving, they said, "Tanya's a lovely girl. She's fortunate to come to a family like yours."

"Oh, *we're* the lucky ones," Jillian said sarcastically.

"We *are* lucky," her dad said firmly. "Tanya's a great kid. She's teaching us as much as we teach her."

"Thanks for the party," said Mr. Woodman. "That Tanya's a charmer. Bring her over to play with Tessie soon, eh?"

"She can be in charge of the plastic bags," Jillian mumbled under her breath.

★

Jillian lay in bed reading about a girl at summer camp, which was exactly where Jillian wished she were. It was late when she heard her mother walking Sharon out to her car.

Jillian settled Chester in their favourite position and shared the thoughts that whirled in her head.

Tanya acted like a Russian princess today. I'm surprised no one gave her a tiara! Such a charmer, so smart, such gorgeous green eyes. Mom and Dad might as well adopt her and send mean, stupid, ugly Jillian back to Belarus.

The next day Sharon took Tanya to the dentist. Jillian and her mother stayed home to play badminton. An hour later, while Jillian was learning to serve, Sharon's car pulled into the driveway.

Mrs. Nelson went to meet them. When she came back she said cheerfully, "Let's practise some more. Sharon's gone home and Tanya's gone to lie down. Poor girl, the freezing is coming out and her mouth hurts."

"She's probably faking," Jillian said, slamming the bird into the net.

"Oh, Jillian," her mother said, dismayed. "How did someone so lucky grow up to be so unkind." Mrs. Nelson walked into the house, shaking her head.

"*Nyet*. No!" Jillian yelled. "Don't touch that!" Tanya stood by Jillian's dresser with her hand on the red music box. Jillian rushed over and shoved hard from behind.

"I'm sick of you. Get out of my room!"

Tanya cringed.

"Out! Out!" Jillian shouted, pointing her finger at the door.

Tanya backed away.

"I can't stand it," Jillian snarled. "I'll show her where she's not welcome."

Jillian lay on the floor and wrote in large letters on a piece of cardboard:

> Jillian Nelson's **Private Room**
> Do not touch my things without permission!
> Do not enter unless you ask first!

Jillian stuck the sign to her door with tape. "There!" She was still looking at it when she heard a noise from behind Tanya's closed door. Crying? No! *Mewing!*

Jillian barged into the room. Tanya sat on her bed with blobs of spot cream on her face, Chester curled contentedly in her arms.

"Leave my cat alone!" Jillian yelled.

"My *kot*," Tanya said, tightening her grasp on Chester and burying her sticky face in his fur.

"He is NOT! Give me my cat!" Jillian screamed, grabbing Chester's hind end. Tanya kept a firm grip on Chester's neck and shoulders. The cat screeched wildly as they struggled back and forth in a fierce tug-of-war that came close to tearing apart the terrified cat.

When Tanya finally let go, Jillian stumbled back, but kept her hold on Chester. At the door, panting for breath, she turned and yelled, "He's *my* cat!"

With his claws digging into Jillian's arms, Chester yowled in pain, terror in his eyes.

★

It was Saturday. Her eyes half closed, Jillian swept her hand over the quilt to feel for Chester, but he wasn't there. The awful memory of his terrified screeching the night before reverberated inside her head.

On her way downstairs, Jillian heard her father in the kitchen. "Here, Tanya. Use this measuring cup to pour the batter."

Jillian detoured, ran out the front door and sat on the top step with her arms wrapped around her waist.

"Breakfast's ready everyone!" her dad called from inside.

Clenching her jaw, Jillian reluctantly took a seat at the table. As her dad put a plate of pancakes in front of her, she reached for the syrup.

"Pass the syrup to other people first, please," Mr. Nelson said.

"I'm sorry, I thought Miss Belarus might like ketchup on her pancakes."

"Not funny," her father said, sending Jillian a sharp look. "So Tanya, how do you like our pancakes?"

"Yes. Thank you, Dad," replied Tanya.

Dad! Jillian jumped up, turned Tanya around so that her face was three inches away and yelled, "Don't you dare call him 'Dad'! He's *my* father! You have to call him 'Mr. Nelson'. There's only one daughter in this house!"

She pushed Tanya away and ran to her bedroom, hurling herself across the bed. Seconds later her father came into the room and sat beside her, reaching for Jillian's hand.

"Jillian, I know you're upset because I made pancakes with Tanya."

Jillian nodded.

"I'm sorry. I thought the fight over Chester last night had exhausted you and I wanted to let you sleep in. I thought making pancakes would be fun for Tanya."

"But *you and I* make the pancakes!"

"You're right. I ought to have waited for you. I'm sorry."

Jillian was surprised. Usually she was the one who had to apologize.

"It's okay … I guess."

"I feel badly that I hurt your feelings."

"I don't like having her here, Dad. I didn't know it would be so hard," Jillian wailed. "I didn't know I'd have to share *everything* — my cat, my toys, my family, my whole life!"

"It's not easy, I know. But Tanya needs us. You might just need her too."

A week of hot summer days went by, but Tanya and Jillian couldn't seem to recapture the fun they'd had before. On a trip to the aquarium Tanya showed no interest in the baby beluga and just when they'd reached the sea otters, who always made Jillian laugh, Tanya wanted to leave. At home, Tanya pushed away the UNO game that she'd used to learn numbers and colours and she shook her head when David invited her to play badminton.

"Why is she so crabby?" Jillian asked her dad.

"Lots of reasons. Those dental appointments have been hard on her and she's still tired and probably missing her family. She's only been here two weeks. It's another six weeks before she goes back to her family."

"That's a long time," Jillian said, more sorry for herself than for Tanya.

★

Tanya was playing Cat's Cradle with her red string on the front steps when Mrs. Nelson invited the girls to come with her for ice cream. Tanya said, "Okay," but looked as though she'd rather be left alone.

Tanya lagged behind on the sidewalk and when they reached a busy corner, Jillian snapped, "Hurry up, Tanya."

Suddenly, Tanya ran past them onto the road, right in front of a car. There was a sharp screech of brakes and an angry shout.

"Tell your daughter to smarten up, lady!"

Mrs. Nelson's face was red. "Sorry," she called to the driver, who accelerated, shaking his head. Mrs. Nelson grabbed Tanya's arm and pulled her back to the sidewalk.

"That's *very* dangerous, Tanya. *Nyet*. You must *not* run onto the road."

Tanya shouted some words in Russian and glared at her, then turned to Jillian and pushed hard with both hands, shoving Jillian backward onto the road. Jillian collapsed over the curb and ended up sprawled in the middle of the street, too shocked to cry.

Mrs. Nelson was shocked too. "You okay?" she asked in a shaky voice, helping Jillian up.

"I think so," Jillian said.

Her mother brushed dirt off Jillian's jeans and turned to Tanya. "You MUST not do that!" she shouted. "That's BAD."

Tanya's mouth trembled and she started to cry. She cried all the way home, Jillian and her mother trailing behind, every thought of ice cream forgotten.

Tanya went to her bedroom and Jillian sat with her mother on the front steps.

"Tanya's so unhappy right now. I just don't have the Russian words to teach her about traffic or anything else. I'm at my wit's end," her mother said, looking distraught.

"Sharon can help you with Russian, Mom. Maybe you should phone her."

"I guess I should," she said wearily, rising to go inside.

Jillian was still sitting on the steps when David came home.

"Tanya pushed me right onto the road and nearly killed me," she said.

"You're exaggerating."

"I am not. You're lucky I'm not dead."

"If you say so, Jillian."

"Let's play badminton. Just you and me?"

"No. You're no fun. If you aren't winning you throw a tantrum and stomp away. I think you've been awful to Tanya. All you think about these days is yourself."

"Somebody has to. Everyone else is thinking about *her*."

"Take a look at yourself, Jillian. Do you like what you see?" He pushed past her into the house.

Jillian found Chester in the backyard and teased him with the badminton bird. When she went inside, her parents were talking sharply to each other as they made dinner.

"Lyn, it doesn't help her learn when she gets yelled at," her dad was saying.

Her mother said, "Then why don't *you* stay home with two warring girls day after day? I'm sick of it. I wish I were back at work."

At dinner nobody looked happy.

"I don't like this clam chowder. It has too much celery in it," Jillian said.

"Oh, it's whine with dinner again, is it?" smirked David.

"You're an ass, David," Jillian said.

"Jillian!" said her parents simultaneously.

"An ass is a donkey. Sorry if that's a problem for you."

"That's no apology," David shouted. "You're always

blurting things out before you think, Big Mouth."

"I don't have a big mouth."

"Yes, you do. It's the size of the Grand Canyon!"

Tanya looked down at her plate, her hands covering her face.

"I can't take any more of this," Mrs. Nelson said. "I'm going over to see Sharon."

"I'm outta here, too," David said. "I'm meeting friends at the park."

Tanya followed him into the hallway where David fixed his hair in front of the hall mirror. She watched as he squeezed gel into his palm and massaged it onto his hair, brushing it straight up to look like freshly mowed grass. He bent both his arms to flex his muscles, grinned in the mirror and turned to make a funny face at Tanya.

Jillian and her dad saw it all from the dining room.

"See how she's always watching David," Jillian said. "She's got a huge crush on him."

As David went out the front door, Jillian called after him, "That hair gel will make you bald. You'll look like Dad before you graduate."

David didn't answer. Her father ran his fingers over the top of his head.

After they cleared the table and cleaned up the kitchen, Mr. Nelson tried to cheer up the girls with one of his old jokes.

"Knock, knock."

"No, Dad!" Jillian protested. "I'm not in the mood."

"Come on. Knock, knock."

"Who's there?" Jillian said, sighing.

"Who?" Tanya echoed.

"One Two."

"One Two who?" Jillian said.

"One Two draw with me tonight?"

Jillian groaned. "That joke was so-o-o bad."

Her dad laughed. Tanya looked puzzled.

"What's 'joke'?"

"It's hard to explain. 'One two' sounds the same as 'want to' …"

Tanya wrinkled her brow.

"Forget it. I'm sick of explaining everything," Jillian said.

Mr. Nelson flashed his daughter a warning look.

"Yes, Dad. We 'one two' draw." Jillian got out paper and felt pens and sat across the dining-room table from Tanya.

"*Flamáster*," Tanya said, holding up a handful of felt pens.

"'Fly master'?" Jillian said, trying to say the word.

Tanya smiled behind her hand at Jillian's pronunciation.

"Dad, she's laughing at me! I'm trying as hard as I can and she's smirking!"

"It did sound odd, Jillian. I know you're trying. Say it again."

"I definitely will not!" Jillian picked up a felt pen. "Look at this! The orange pen is completely dry. Tanya never puts the tops back on. How can I make a good picture without good pens?"

She picked up a black pen, looked at the matted top and hurled it aside. "All the pens are wrecked! Tanya presses too hard. She's hopeless," Jillian said, glaring at Tanya.

Jillian picked up a handful of pens, lifted them over her head and sent them flying against the dining-room window.

"Belarus brat!" she screamed in Tanya's face.

Tanya ran upstairs.

Mr. Nelson took his daughter by the shoulders. "Jillian Nelson. That behaviour is not acceptable."

Jillian stared back defiantly.

"Jillian, you are the one who begged this family to invite Tanya into our home. And you are the one treating her badly."

"She's not the girl I wanted."

"Well, Tanya's the girl we've got! You'd better learn to get along with her. Now, go to your room and think about how you're going to do that."

"That's not fair. I thought we were going to draw together."

"Go to your room RIGHT NOW!"

Thumping up the stairs, Jillian called, "Remember, *I'm* the one who picked up dog poop for that girl!"

Jillian was lying on her bed when she heard voices downstairs. Her mother was back. Jillian got out of bed and eavesdropped on the rest of her family as she leaned against the wall on the upstairs landing.

"You know what? I don't even like my sister these days," David said. "She's being a total jerk."

"It's not only Jillian. Tanya's misbehaving too," her dad said. "Last week the two of them nearly tore the cat apart and today Tanya could have hurt Jillian seriously by pushing her onto the road."

Jillian's mother added, "I told Sharon I feel like a failure. I'm a professional mediator. I'm supposed to help people solve conflicts, but right now these two girls are beyond me."

"What did Sharon say?" Mr. Nelson asked.

"She said children who aren't sure of themselves often feel jealous when their visitors get attention. She thinks Jillian just needs confidence."

Jillian's father said, "I feel badly we haven't helped her to feel more confident."

Her mother sounded on the edge of tears. "We're her parents. It must be our fault."

Jillian slumped against the wall. It wasn't her parents' fault. It was her own fault. The whole summer was one big mistake.

SEVEN

"Let's go for a walk, Jillian," her dad said the next morning.

It was three blocks to the beach and this Sunday in July was one of those clear summer days when the breeze off the sea blew cool and clean against her face. When they reached the stone steps leading down to the shore they took off their runners and headed west along the beach, dangling their shoes by the laces.

The tide was halfway out and the sand was like warm silk against Jillian's feet. The tall buildings of the city were set out like chess pieces across the bay and, on the north shore, the mountains rose, deep blue, almost indigo, against the bright sky. Noisy gulls cried to each other as they swooped and circled over the water.

"Five freighters today," Jillian said.

"Look at the white sailboat skimming around them," her father added.

Jillian looked across the water. "And a bald eagle!"

"Where?" asked her dad, scanning the sky. "I can't see it."

"You, Dad! You!" Jillian chortled.

"Good one," he laughed, checking the top of his head.

Empty mussel shells formed a deep mound against the log where they sat down. Gentle waves, like cat's tongues, licked the edge of the sand. The smell of seaweed, sour and hot, drifted toward them in the heat.

"Remember how hard you worked to convince us to bring over a girl from Belarus?" said her dad.

"It was a big mistake," Jillian said staring at the sailboat.

"I don't think so. Because of you, we're making a difference in Tanya's life."

"Yeah, for the worse."

"It's been hard, but Tanya's looking healthier these days. She doesn't need as much sleep and the sores on her face are almost gone."

"But I'm bored looking up words in the dictionary. I'm tired of her coming into my room and touching my things."

Jillian's father nodded. "I wish she didn't climb all over me when I get home from the office."

Jillian looked surprised. She thought her dad liked *everything* about Tanya.

He went on. "Your mother would prefer not to have

extra work. David would be relieved not to have two squabbling girls in the house."

"Chester would like it if we didn't fight over him," Jillian added.

"Right. But things don't go smoothly just because we'd like them to. We have to *make* things work."

"I don't know how," Jillian said, digging in the sand with her feet.

"Try putting yourself in Tanya's shoes."

"I'm not putting myself in her horrible old shoes."

"Just try to understand what she must be feeling."

"I know how I feel when she puts herself in my party shoes."

"How *do* you feel?"

"I feel mad at her ... for butting into my life."

Jillian looked down where her bare toes had tunnelled through to a cold, wet layer of sand.

Her father spoke quietly. "But we invited Tanya into our lives. Now it's up to us to figure out how we can get along. It's a big challenge."

"I don't want a challenge. I want a friend."

"You'll have a friend, if you can *be* one."

"I can't. It's too hard."

Jillian slid off the log to lie on her stomach in the sand. Her eyes closed. The sun was hot on the back of her legs. She could almost fall asleep.

She pictured Tanya: thin and frightened at the airport; the tender look on her face when she held Chester; her crazy laughter when she put the toast on her head; her big grin the first time she rode the bike.

Tanya was like every other kid; she just wanted someone to play with. She wanted … a friend. Jillian knew
that feeling; she'd learned it well in 6B.

She lifted her head, leaned on her elbow in the
sand and picked up a dark-blue mussel shell. It was the
size and shape of a baby's cupped hand and was
encrusted with sand. Jillian pried it open to see inside.
To her surprise, the two inside halves were like irides-
cent palms, glowing pearly white and streaked with
hints of pink and turquoise. She ran her finger over the
smooth surface, marvelling at the luminous secret
hidden inside such an ordinary shell.

She was slipping the two half-shells into the pocket
of her shorts when her father asked, "How about lunch
at that new fish-and-chip place up the beach?"

Ten minutes later they were sitting at the counter.
Jillian said, "If Tanya were here she'd pour half a bottle
of ketchup on these chips."

"Never seen a kid so crazy about the stuff."

Jillian was quiet for a minute. "There's just one
thing. Is she allowed to call you 'Dad'?"

"No. That's something only you and David can do.
I'll ask Tanya to call me Mark."

"That's what I thought you'd say."

Jillian was quiet on the walk home. Back in the house,
she picked up the dictionary to find the word she
needed.

Tanya was sitting on her bed making a necklace;

coloured beads were spread all over the quilt.

Pointing to herself, Jillian said, "*Druk*, Tanya?"

Tanya looked up, surprised.

"Yes, *druk*." Jillian nodded. "I want to be your friend."

"*Da. Druk*," Tanya said, patting the side of the bed next to her. "Frie-nd."

Jillian felt a wave of relief and sat down on the plastic beads, then jumped up as they pricked the back of her legs. Tanya reached over and brushed her off, sending beads cascading onto the floor.

Suddenly Jillian grinned. She had a *druk*! A *druk*!

The next day Mrs. Nelson gave the girls two big scrapbooks and double copies of the photographs she'd taken.

"Thought you might like to record your summer memories," she said.

Tanya and Jillian sat at the picnic table in the backyard with crayons, scissors and glue.

Tanya wrote CANADA in big letters on the cover of her scrapbook. Underneath she coloured a Canadian flag. Inside she drew a picture of the house on the hill and another of Chester with his tail in the air.

Jillian wrote MY SUMMER WITH TANYA on the cover of her scrapbook. On the first page she wrote about meeting Tanya at the airport; then she picked out photographs of Tanya waving from the front seat of the car and Tanya with her new haircut, taken the day Jillian decided to let her hair grow long.

Tanya finished cutting out a picture from a magazine and held up the bottle of glue, which had sparkles, like stars, suspended in it.

"David!" she said, taking off the orange lid and squeezing a blob of thick goo onto the back of her picture.

Jillian laughed. It *did* look like David's hair gel. Then she laughed again as Tanya pasted a picture of a Canadian bathroom into her scrapbook.

Later that week, the girls walked to the mall to spend their allowances. Tanya jingled three loonies in her new purse.

"Plenty of money," she said, quoting *The Owl and the Pussycat*. "In Canada, dollars. In Belarus, rubles."

"In England a 'five pound note'!" Jillian added.

A magic show was going on near the fountain. When it was over they walked up and down the corridors of the mall so Tanya could study every window display.

"So many things," she said. "In Belarus, not so many."

Tanya lingered in front of a display window full of shoes.

"So many *túfli*," she said, her eyes wide.

Jillian guessed that Belarusians made their shoes last a long time. It was only last week Tanya had finally exchanged her worn canvas shoes for runners.

At the drugstore Jillian spent her money on strawberry licorice and lipgloss. Tanya bought three postcards of Vancouver and a small maple-leaf pin, then asked to share Jillian's candy.

Jillian taped a new sign to her bedroom door and stood back to admire it.

Just as she was scrunching up the old sign for the recycling bin, Jillian heard the clunk of the mail slot and ran to the front door. On the hall floor lay an envelope with Tanya's name on it and a pale blue stamp with a picture of a factory.

"Letter for you, Tanya!" she called.

Tanya ran up to her bedroom to read the letter. She'd been with the Nelsons more than three weeks now and this was the first letter from home.

The family went about the morning chores. David and Jillian cleaned their rooms; Mrs. Nelson did the laundry. It was another hot day and they were going to the beach that afternoon.

When Mrs. Nelson called them for lunch, Tanya's door stayed closed. Behind it, Jillian heard Tanya crying. When she got closer, the crying sounded like choking.

Jillian knocked and opened the door a crack. Tanya lay on the bed, her knees curled up, her face blotchy, pages of the letter clutched in both hands.

Jillian was not sure what to do, but she knew a *druk* would stay nearby, so she sat with her hand resting on Tanya's leg, waiting. Then she went to the bathroom and got a wet facecloth to wipe Tanya's swollen eyes. The letter must have terrible news.

"Is it your *máma*?" said Jillian.

Tanya shook her head.

"Your *pápa*?"

Tanya shook her head again; giving Jillian such a forlorn look that she thought her heart would break.

"Mariana," Tanya said in a weak voice.

"Your sister?" Jillian said. "What's wrong with her?"

"*Balná*."

Jillian grabbed the dictionary. Mariana was sick!

Jillian rushed to tell her mother. As soon as she heard, Mrs. Nelson telephoned Sharon and asked her to come over after work.

When she arrived, Sharon talked quietly to Tanya in the living room while the family waited in the kitchen.

Finally, Sharon invited the Nelsons to join them and told them what was in the letter. "Mariana has been diagnosed with leukaemia. She'd been having back-aches and losing weight. They've taken her to the best hospital in Minsk for treatment."

Tanya's chin quivered.

"Oh, that's terrible, Tanya," Jillian said, putting her

cool hand against Tanya's hot face.

"I'm so sorry, Tanya," Mrs. Nelson said.

"Mariana must have chemotherapy every day for twenty-six days and then she'll continue medication at home. Her cell count will be checked every month for three years. The doctor says she's hopeful the treatment will cure Mariana."

Tanya was breathing quickly and she spoke to Sharon in a shaky voice. Sharon translated for the family. "Tanya tells me she's heard that children can die from leukaemia."

Jillian looked at Tanya. "She knows about things I've never heard of," she said.

Sharon said, "I'm trying to reassure Tanya that doctors have great success treating childhood leukaemia these days."

As she was leaving, Sharon said, "Please phone me anytime and I'll come over to translate. It's hard on children when they can't talk about their feelings in their own language."

"I will," Mrs. Nelson said. "You've been a big help."

That night Tanya went to bed early.

"Here's someone to keep you company," said Jillian, tucking the amber bear under Tanya's quilt. "*Druk*," she whispered.

"Friends," Tanya answered.

As she lay in her own bed, Jillian heard a whimpering sound from Tanya's room, a sound unlike anything she'd heard before.

★

The next morning Jillian asked Tanya, "*Pismó pisát*? Would you like to write a letter?"

Tanya nodded and Jillian asked her mother for her best writing paper, the kind with a border of pale roses and envelopes to match. Leaning over Tanya's shoulder, Jillian watched as she filled the page with strange letters and strokes: *N* and *R* were backward, there were stars, *B*s with tails and upside-down *U*s on little stands.

"That's the Cyrillic alphabet. It has thirty-three letters, many quite different from the twenty-six letters in the Roman alphabet," Jillian's mother said.

While Tanya wrote, Jillian sat beside her, working on a drawing of their Vancouver house on the hill. She put Chester on the front steps and Tanya, David, Jillian and her parents peering out from each of the windows.

"For Mariana," Jillian said, handing the drawing to Tanya.

"*Spasíba*," Tanya replied, carefully folding the drawing and putting it into the envelope.

★

For a couple of days Tanya seemed more cheerful, but on the third day she turned into a different person.

"I can't figure out what's wrong," Jillian said to her father. "I thought Tanya felt better after we'd mailed the letter, but now she won't watch a video with me and she turned her back when I offered to read to her.

I thought she liked it when we read together."

"I'm sure it's because she can't stop thinking about Mariana," he said. "Give her some space."

After supper Jillian went into her bedroom to get a book. As always, her eyes drifted around the room to her animals and CDs lined up on the shelf, to her pictures on the wall, to her dresser with … Jillian's heart missed a beat. The red velvet music box was tipped on its side!

She rushed to the dresser, put the box upright and held her breath as she turned the key. The lid opened, the velvet platform slid up and, as always, the fairy turned to the music, one arm bent gracefully at the shoulder, but where the other arm should have been … only an ugly stub remained!

Jillian looked around in panic. At the back of the dresser she saw something small and pink — the tiny broken arm still holding the wand.

"Mom! Dad!" she yelled.

Immediately, both her parents appeared at Jillian's door.

Jillian pointed dramatically to the tiny pink arm and the stub at the fairy's shoulder.

"My fairy is mutilated! And I know who did it! Tanya! She came into my room and broke it. She's ruined the most beautiful thing I own. She broke it on purpose!" Jillian blurted.

"I'm very sorry the fairy's arm is broken," Jillian's mother said. "But if Tanya did it, it must have been an accident. I'm sure she feels awful."

Mr. Nelson left the room and came back with Tanya, whose whole body was trembling.

"Tanya, did you play with the music box and break it?"

"Sorry! Sorry!" she wailed, burying her head in Mr. Nelson's sleeve.

"I told you she did it!" screamed Jillian, raising her arm and moving toward Tanya. "I hate you! I'd like to smash you just like you smashed the fairy. You … Belarusian!"

"Stop," her mother said, taking a firm hold of Jillian's arm. "Jillian, do not threaten Tanya." Her mother's voice was stern. "Tanya was wrong to play with your music box when you'd asked her not to, but she's already told you she's sorry. What more do you want?"

"You're taking her side!" Jillian straightened her shoulders and looked at Tanya. "I'm *not* sorry Mariana is sick. I hope she dies."

Jillian's words were like rocks hurled through the air and a terrible silence hung around them until her mother spoke.

"Jillian Margaret Nelson! Don't you dare say that to anyone! EVER! Do you hear me?"

Jillian's hair fell across her face as she looked sideways at her mother.

Mrs. Nelson was shaking. "Tanya may not understand your words, but the rest of us do. Being upset does not give you the right to be cruel!"

Her father was pale. "Just look at this girl, Jillian. She knows exactly what you said."

Tanya's head was lowered and her shoulders heaved.

"Say you're sorry," Mr. Nelson said to Jillian.

"I won't! I'm not sorry," Jillian yelled, hurling herself face down on her bed and pulling the pillow over her head.

After Mrs. Nelson took Tanya to her bedroom, Jillian's father marched over to the bed. "Look at me, Jillian. I want to talk to you. LOOK AT ME!"

Slowly Jillian rolled over, pulled at the hair stuck to her hot cheeks and lay with her arms crossed defiantly over her chest.

"Jillian, the fairy's arm can be glued back on, but you have broken something far more precious than Tanya has. You've broken a very fragile trust between the two of you and you will have to work hard to rebuild it," her father said.

Jillian said nothing. Her eyes were sore and her throat ached.

"Stay in your room. Maybe by the morning you'll have sorted out what you should do."

Jillian rolled back onto her stomach and sobbed into her pillow. She wept for the ruined music box and for her ruined summer, but most of all, she wept for herself.

Later, Jillian's father returned to her room. He went to the dresser, picked up the china arm and put it inside the music box, then headed out the door. "Night, Jillian."

"Night, Dad."

Jillian's mother came and sat on the bed a few minutes later.

"How am I going to tell Gram?" Jillian asked.

"You can phone in the morning. She'll understand. Gram's had to cope with a lot of things since Grandpa died. I don't think a broken music box will feel like the end of the world."

Jillian sighed and her mother went on. "Like Tanya, Gram misses someone far away. I do too. I miss my father, your grandpa. There are so many times I've wanted to tell him about you and David and I can't."

Just then, Chester padded into the room and jumped onto the bed.

"Need a warm cat for company tonight?" her mom said.

"I do," Jillian said in a small voice, wrapping her exhausted arms around Chester while her mother tucked her in.

"The fairy is broken forever, Mom. I just know it."

"Maybe not. Lots of things can be fixed."

Jillian lay in the dark. Her chest ached as she heard her own words echo in the room.

I'm not sorry Mariana is sick. I hope she dies.

EIGHT

It was a new day — a fresh start.

Mrs. Nelson was sitting at the breakfash table.

"I phoned Gram about the music box, Mom, and she said to remember that things are never as important as people. She's invited Tanya and me for a sleepover Friday night."

"Great. Now look on Dad's desk," her mother said. "He left something for you."

Jillian picked up the music box. She hesitated, scared to turn the key, but when the lid opened, there was the fairy, whole again, with the mended arm holding up the wand. When she looked closely at the fairy's shoulder, Jillian could see a line as fine as a thread where the break had been. It would show only if you knew where to look.

"I wish I could take back the words I said to Tanya," Jillian said.

"You can't take those words back, Jillian, but you can put other words in their place. Actions, too."

"I have an idea. Can I have the white wicker tray you use to bring me breakfast in bed when I'm sick?"

Her mother found the tray and two pink cloth napkins. Jillian spread a napkin as a placemat; then she folded the other into a triangle and placed a spoon and knife on the side. She poured a glass of orange juice and put her favourite Peter Rabbit egg cup on a blue plate.

Jillian boiled an egg — three minutes from the time the water boiled — and made two slices of brown toast, cut them in fingers and put them on the tray beside a small jar of Gram's strawberry jam.

Humming the music box song, she walked upstairs, balancing the tray carefully as she knocked on Tanya's door.

"*Da*. Come." The voice sounded shaky.

"Breakfast!"

"For me?" Tanya stared at the tray.

She looked so regal sitting up in bed with the breakfast tray on her lap that Jillian had to smile. Tanya smiled back.

It was amazing how much you could say with a smile, but still, Jillian needed words. "Tanya, I'm sorry."

Looking dismayed, Tanya repeated, "I'm sorry, sorry."

"No," said Jillian, her hand on her own chest. "*I'm*

the one who has to apologize. Breaking the fairy was an accident. What I said wasn't."

Maybe Tanya couldn't understand every word, but her expression showed she knew what Jillian was trying to say.

"Now eat your toast fingers," Jillian said, teaching Tanya to dip them into the creamy egg yolk. "I'll be right back."

When she first saw the music box Tanya looked stricken.

"Look!" Jillian said. The music started and there was the fairy holding the wishing star in the air.

"Isn't it great!" Jillian exclaimed.

"*Da*. Yes!" Tanya said.

Jillian handed Tanya the music box and motioned for her to wind the key. Very, very carefully, Tanya turned the key and, once again, the girls watched the fairy pirouette.

When you wish upon a star
Makes no difference who you are,
Anything your heart desires
will come to you.

There was something more Jillian wanted. She had to tell Tanya that she understood how scary it was that Mariana had leukaemia. Jillian picked up the dictionary. What were the right words? Not "I'm believing." Not quite "I'm hoping."

By the time Tanya dipped the last toast finger in

the strawberry jam, Jillian had an idea. She pointed to the fairy's star. "*Zvezdá zhelániy*. Wishing star."

"*Da*, wishing star," repeated Tanya.

"I wished for you to come to Canada and it worked. Let's wish for Mariana to get better."

"*Da*. For Mariana," Tanya said, closing her eyes and holding up her arm, her finger pointed in the air.

Tanya came out of the dentist's office with the widest grin they'd ever seen. The stains on her teeth were gone.

"No charge. It's my pleasure," said Dr. Bridge, waving goodbye.

As soon as they pulled into the driveway, Mrs. Nelson rushed for her camera.

The two girls put their heads together. Jillian made the *V* sign with her fingers behind Tanya's head.

"The kid's got a great smile," David said.

"She sure has," Jillian said, her arm around Tanya's shoulders, unaware of the *V* sign behind her.

David was looking after the girls while Mrs. Nelson went for lunch with Sharon.

"We don't need babysitting, David," Jillian said. "Eleven year olds are perfectly capable of looking after themselves."

"That's a joke, right?"

Jillian and Tanya decided to paint their nails. Their

thumbs would have red circles like a bull's eye; their pointer fingers would be blue with a yellow star; the next finger, half green and half blue; the fourth, yellow and black bumblebee stripes; and finally, the little finger, fluorescent pink.

"Pinkie finger," said Jillian, wiggling it to demonstrate.

"Toast finger," said Tanya.

When their nails were dry, the girls called to David, "Get ready. We're cooking lunch."

They emptied a package of macaroni dinner into a saucepan, then added water, a tin of tuna and half a jar of green olives. The heat made the mixture the consistency of porridge. They added more water, way too much, and had to serve the meal in soup bowls.

"*Chut-chut smeshnóy*," said Tanya, carrying a bowl to David.

"What's that mean?" David asked doubtfully.

"It means 'a little bit funny'," Jillian said, laughing as she showed David the words in the dictionary.

"This is NOT *chut-chut smeshnóy*, Tanya! You're trying to poison me," David said, staring at the olives floating in the macaroni and cheese.

Tanya was on her toes, searching in a cupboard.

"What are you looking for?" Jillian asked.

"It's red," Tanya said, shaking her hand up and down.

David shrugged. "I give."

"She wants ketchup," Jillian said on her way to the fridge.

"This concoction needs more than ketchup," David said, pushing away his bowl.

Tanya smiled and, one by one, picked out olives with her painted fingers and slurped them into her mouth.

The next weekend the girls worked on their scrapbooks. Jillian wrote: *I told Tanya we were taking a boat to Victoria and she said, "A pea-green boat?" I told her, "No, a big white ferry boat!"*

Tanya glued postcards of the ferry, the Undersea Gardens and totem poles at the Royal Museum into her scrapbook. As she squeezed out the glitter glue, she started to giggle.

"Come," she said, leading Jillian to the bathroom. She pointed to David's bottle of hair gel, held up the bottle of glue and raised her eyebrows.

"Excellent!"

"Big night tonight. I'm going to a party," David called on his way to the shower.

When he sat down for supper, the girls had to look away to keep from laughing.

Right after the meal David went to the hall mirror and started fixing his hair. The yowl he let out could have been heard by the Leylands across the street. He roared down the hallway, his fingers stuck to his hair, which was layered with gobs of sparkling goo.

"What is it? What the heck is it? What's happened to my hair?" he yelled. He pounded up and down, his face contorted, elbows flapping, hands pulling at his hair. "This stuff is HARDENING," David bellowed, trying to free his hands without yanking out his hair.

Tanya and Jillian slid to the floor, clutching their stomachs and laughing uncontrollably.

"What's going on?" Mrs. Nelson asked, poking her head around the kitchen door.

"*Chut-chut smeshnóy,*" Tanya shouted.

"Yeah, just a little bit funny!" Jillian shrieked. "It's only glue."

"It's glue? My hair is GLUED?"

One hand broke free as David lurched toward the girls. Ropey goop hung from his fingers as he grabbed for them.

"Ugh! Don't touch us!" Jillian screamed as she and Tanya covered their heads. Chester scurried out of the room and up the stairs.

"Calm down, David." Mrs. Nelson tried to speak, but she was overcome with laughter. "It will … wash … out."

As Mr. Nelson came inside from watering the lawn, he saw his son stumbling toward him, one hand twisted in the air and the other firmly attached to his glistening head.

"The brats put glue — glue with sparkles — in my hair gel! They're … laughing at me. Do something, Dad!"

David stared at his father in disbelief. "Dad! It's not funny."

★

"He's been in the bathroom a long time," Jillian said.

Eventually, David came down the hall. He wore a clean shirt and his hair looked almost normal.

"Please sit down, David. We need to talk about this," Mrs. Nelson said in her best mediator's voice. "This glue incident … is … not funny." She paused, but she couldn't help herself. She burst into gales of laughter again.

David shook his head in disgust. Actually, Jillian noticed with fascination, David's head shook but his hair stayed still.

"Sorry, David," his mother said, gaining control of herself. "But it really was funny. Though a bit unkind."

"It was Jillian's idea," David said, glaring at his sister.

"Tanya gets good ideas, too, you know," Jillian said.

"It was your idea, Tanya?" David said.

"Yep."

"But Jillian went along with it?"

"Yep," said Jillian.

"Interesting," David said, heading for the door.

"Can't you stick around while …" Mrs. Nelson caught herself.

"Give a guy a break. And give me a chance to get even!" he said, making a grab for Tanya, who jumped up and ran to the backyard.

NINE

"Can we swim in the pool first?" Jillian asked as they pulled up to Gram's apartment building. "Why not!" Gram answered.

While Gram swam lengths, the girls practised a synchronized swimming routine. When they were ready with a show, Gram sat on the side and watched.

With smooth easy strokes the girls swam the front crawl up the pool, heads held high, then turned onto their backs and put one leg, then the other up in the air, toes pointed. They did a reverse somersault and surfaced, toes touching, three times, then raised their crossed arms and waved like Olympic stars.

"I love it," Gram said. "Do it again, then I'll get supper."

While Gram prepared chicken in the kitchen, the

girls sat on the sofa and looked through the family photo album.

"Somewhere in those photographs, Jillian, is the one of your grandfather holding you right after you were born. See if you can find it."

Jillian turned the pages and found the picture: a handsome man wearing a white shirt stood in a garden cradling a baby wrapped in a shawl.

"That's the one," Gram said, looking over her shoulder. "What I remember about that picture is the look in your grandpa's eyes as he held you.

Jillian studied the picture. She saw the look.

After supper, Gram cut big pieces of watermelon and set three chairs out on the balcony. As they spat the seeds into a saucepan, Gram asked Tanya about Mariana.

Using her dictionary, Tanya explained that Mariana liked to read and that she helped with Tanya's homework.

"I'd like to sew something for Mariana. Can you find out how big she is?" Gram asked Jillian.

"*Bolsháya* Mariana?" Jillian asked, placing a hand on each side of Tanya's waist.

Tanya shook her head. "*Ménshe*."

Jillian moved her hands closer together. "Like this?"

"*Ménshe*," Tanya said, looking sad.

Jillian moved her hands even closer together. "Mariana is much smaller than Tanya, Gram."

"Poor girl," Gram said.

"Chernobyl," Tanya said, looking up at Gram.

Tanya asked for some paper and drew a large square building with a tall smokestack. Then she stood in front of Gram and Jillian and threw her hands up in the air.

"Boom … boom … BOOM!"

"The explosion! She's telling us what happened, Gram," Jillian said.

"But Tanya wasn't born until after the accident."

"She knows all about it. Sharon told us all the kids in Belarus do."

Tanya began to shape a house in the air with her hands. "*Máma's* and *Pápa's dom*," she said. Then she held her hands high and lowered them slowly, her fingers waving like falling snow.

"It's fallout. After the explosion radioactive dust fell from the sky onto her parents' house."

"Mariana would have been a baby then," Gram said, her usually cheerful face looking grave.

"Tanya and I have a secret, Gram. Want to hear it?" Jillian asked.

"You know I love secrets."

"We've wished on a star, the music box fairy's star wand. We wished for Mariana to get better."

"*Sekrét*," said Tanya, putting her finger to her lips and looking at Gram.

Gram looked a little brighter. "Perhaps for a secret that big we need a bigger wand. Let's make one!"

She collected everything they needed and sat with the girls at the table. "First, cut a big star out of this cardboard and tape it to my wooden mixing spoon."

Jillian watched Tanya as she concentrated on

cutting the heavy cardboard.

"Now, take some foil and wrap it over the star."

The girls made a fat silver star and when they finished, Gram stood up, held the wand above her head and, with the grace of a fairy queen, tapped the tops of their heads.

"We wish for Mariana to get better soon," she said.

In the morning Gram cooked waffles and, after they'd eaten, brought two parcels from her bedroom.

"This is a little gift to your *bábushka* from me," Gram said, giving a parcel to Tanya. Folded in tissue paper was a soft linen handkerchief embroidered with wildflowers.

"*Spasíba, Baba*," Tanya said.

"The box is for you, Jillian."

Jillian slowly opened the box. Inside a silver picture frame was the photograph of a handsome man in a white shirt cradling a baby.

Gram said, "I've been saving that frame for you, Jillian, and last night I took the photograph out of my album. You should have it."

Jillian stared at the picture and when she looked up she saw that Gram had tears in her eyes, too.

An hour later, as Gram drove the girls home, the star wand on the seat beside them, they passed a bank and Tanya called from the seat, "*Bába*. Let's get money!"

"Tanya loves the bank machines," Jillian explained. "She can't believe money comes out when Mom puts in her card."

"Neither can I," said Gram.

Farther on, near a familiar corner, Tanya called out again, "*Bába*. Wash the car!"

"She doesn't mean to be bossy, Gram, but she likes going through the car wash."

"Okay. My wagon could do with a scrub!" Gram laughed.

That weekend Jillian and Tanya rode their bikes to the beach. They sat on a log and looked across to the mountains on the north shore.

"I know a First Nations legend about the mountains," Jillian said. "It's told by the poet Pauline Johnson and I read it in school this year."

Jillian pointed to the two tall peaks next to each other.

"The Two Sisters. *Dva Syóstry*," she said. "A long time ago, two native sisters wanted to stop the fighting between tribes, so they begged their father, the chief, to invite an enemy tribe from the north to feast with them. The chief agreed and everyone got together. The tribes have been friendly toward each other ever since. Now, when we see the Two Sisters we think of friendship."

"*Dva Syóstry*," Tanya said, looking up at the peaks.

The girls lay on their backs in the warm sand.

"Do this," Jillian said, moving her arms to draw wings in the sand. "In Ottawa I made snow angels. Here we can make sand fairies."

As they got on their bikes, Jillian saw Molly and Gail wading in the water down the beach. She could have waved, but decided not to. She wondered why Jasmine wasn't with them.

A few nights later, while Mr. and Mrs. Nelson were out for a walk, David appeared on the porch with two glass bowls of vanilla ice cream topped with thick red sauce and whole strawberries.

"Awesome, David," Jillian said.

Tanya dug in deeply with her spoon, a second ahead of Jillian, but the warning look on Tanya's face didn't come soon enough.

Both girls opened their eyes wide in shock. Their lips puckered and twisted to expel the red-and-white mixture.

"Blah! Bluh! Ugh!" the girls spluttered into the air. Sauce dripped over their chins. They shook their heads, trying to banish the foul-tasting mix of sweet strawberries, cold vanilla ice cream — and ketchup.

"Blah!" grimaced Tanya, wiping her mouth with her T-shirt to get rid of the thick sauce.

"It's disgusting!" Jillian bent over the porch railing to spit into the flower bed below. "Gross! I can still taste it."

"Ketchup. Yuck!" said Tanya, screwing up her face.

"Revenge, sweet revenge," David chuckled.

The picnic for all the Belarusian children and their families started at eleven o'clock Saturday morning, but as they were getting ready David said, "Count me out. Too many little kids."

"Come with us," his mother said. "Harrison Lake is perfect for swimming this time of year and there'll be older kids around."

"Come on, Big Guy! You might meet a nice girl," Jillian said.

"Not with my luck."

Tanya grabbed David's arm, dragging him toward the front door. "Come, Big Guy!"

David had to laugh. "Okay, okay. I'll go, Tanya, but wait 'til I get my suit and towel."

When they reached the lake, families were spreading blankets and putting their picnic baskets down on the grass. Jillian looked around and, to her surprise, saw Jasmine nearby. She was with a girl from Belarus.

Jasmine wore a bright yellow bathing suit and her dark hair was pulled back in a heavy ponytail that swung from shoulder to shoulder as she walked toward Jillian.

"Hi!" Jasmine said. "I can't believe it! Have you got someone from Belarus staying with you too?"

"Yes. Tanya's over there in the green-striped bathing suit, sitting with my family. I didn't know you were part of the program. I didn't see you at the airport."

"It was late, so my mother and I stayed home and

my father picked up Nina. Nina's the girl wearing glasses, talking to my mother. The first week she was with us I noticed she couldn't see things in the distance, so we took her to our optometrist for glasses. Now she can see everything, including her brother!"

Jasmine smiled and pointed to a boy about eight being chased toward them by a tall girl.

"Meet Nicole and Sasha," Jasmine said. "Sasha is Nina's brother and he's staying with Nicole." Sasha, a pale skinny boy, clung to Nicole, who had long blond hair and was wearing shorts and a haltertop.

"Hi," Jillian said.

"Remember me, Nicole?" said David coming up behind them.

"Sure I do. Biology class last year, right?" Nicole said.

"Right," David said, brushing his hand quickly over his hair.

"How's it been having a girl from Belarus live with you?" Nicole asked Jillian.

"It was hard at first," Jillian answered. "Tanya was tired and jet-lagged when she arrived."

"Sasha too. He's so little and he was really homesick," Nicole said. "At first, Jasmine brought his sister over every day."

Jillian looked at Jasmine. "Why didn't you tell the class that you were having a girl stay with you?"

"You know how it is. I didn't want anyone to think I was bragging," Jasmine said. "But if I'd known you were hosting someone we could have done things together."

"I should have told you about Tanya."

"Why didn't you?" Jasmine asked.

"I wanted to surprise everyone and bring Tanya the last day of school. Nobody in 6B was very friendly so …"

"We would have been your friends, but we thought *you* didn't like *us*. You acted so stuck-up."

"Why did you think that?"

"You were always saying everything was better in Ottawa, like, you'd been learning French since grade one … You made us feel stupid."

"I didn't mean to," Jillian said. "I was just nervous about being in a new school."

"But you said 6B girls were ignorant."

Jillian's face burned. "I blurt things out sometimes."

"That's my sister!" David said.

Nicole turned to Jillian. "You know what, Jillian? Sometimes I blurt things out, too."

Jillian looked up at Nicole gratefully.

"So," Nicole asked, "is Tanya as crazy about ketchup as all the other kids from Belarus?"

"Yep, but I gave her a ketchup sundae as a joke and I think I've cured her," David said.

"You didn't!" Nicole giggled, flipping her long hair over her shoulder with the back of her hand.

Tanya came over and asked them to join the rest of the children, who'd gathered in the shade of a big tree. The group spread out to make the circle larger and Jillian met Anya, Yulia, Olga and the three Canadian children sponsoring them. Sasha sat beside his sister

Nina, who wore glasses that seemed too big for her narrow face.

Russian words bounced back and forth and, for the first time, Jillian understood what it must have been like for Tanya. The words came so fast. She felt left out and exhausted.

Tanya looked over at Jillian. "Now English," she said and the children talked together as best they could.

"Vancouver is big." "Chaussy is small." "No mountains in Chaussy." "Canada is nice." "Going home."

In a little while, Nicole said, "Let's swim," and they waded into the lake. Nicole and David swam together out to the raft and the girls played water tag with Sasha.

Afterward, eating egg sandwiches, Mrs. Nelson said to Jillian, "Who are those two girls who came over to talk to you?"

"Jasmine's from 6B and Nicole goes to David's school. They're nice," Jillian said.

"Very nice," added David.

After lunch there was a baseball game. David taught the Belarusian kids how to hold the bat and when to swing. Nicole showed them how to stay on the bases and tag a runner out.

"It's good! I like it!" Tanya yelled to Jillian as she slid into home plate.

"Safe!" Mr. Nelson declared.

As the Nelsons were packing to go home, Jasmine came over and introduced her parents. Jasmine's mother, Amrit Sandhu, wore a blue sari and had dark hair pulled back to the nape of her neck.

"We met at the orientation meeting," she said to the Nelsons.

"How's your summer going?" asked Simran Sandhu, Jasmine's father.

"I can't say it hasn't had its difficult moments," said Jillian's mother, laughing.

The Sandhus nodded and Jillian's father added, "Fortunately we seem to be on track now."

Jasmine's father turned to a tall woman standing nearby. "Let me introduce Louise Johnson, Nicole's mother and Sasha's host."

"Hi, everybody," Louise said. "Quite a summer, isn't it? I don't know how Nicole and I would have managed without the Sandhus. I'm a single parent with a busy medical practice and we've really leaned on them to help Sasha adjust."

"We're all in this together," said Jasmine's mother.

When it was time to leave, the families separated to load up their cars.

"*Paká*," Tanya called, waving to the kids from Belarus.

"*Paká, Paká,*" they called back.

"*Paká* means 'See you,'" Jasmine explained.

"Well, *paká*, Jasmine," Jillian said.

On the way home, Mrs. Nelson turned around in her seat and asked, "Have a good time, Tanya?"

"*Bolshóy dóbra,*" Tanya answered.

"A big good!" David said, laughing. "I agree."

"You've got the right words, Tanya," Jillian said, flipping her hair with the back of her hand.

TEN

As the Nelsons' car rounded the corner on the way back from the picnic, they saw Mrs. Leyland kneeling in the middle of the road. They drove closer and realized she was bending over a cat.

Chester!

Mr. Nelson pulled the car to the curb and the girls raced over. It was a terrible sight: Chester lay motionless, his chest barely rising, his fur matted with blood and his eyes flickering wildly.

"It just happened. Hit and run," Mrs. Leyland said in a shaky voice. "I rushed out the minute I heard the brakes."

"No! Chester! Chester!" Jillian wailed, clutching Tanya who was sobbing.

"Hush a minute, girls," Mrs. Nelson said. "I think I heard a faint meow."

Like turning off a tap, Tanya and Jillian stopped crying and listened. There it was again — a barely audible meow.

"Chester's not dying!" Jillian exclaimed.

David ran to get a beach towel from the car. Mr. Nelson lifted Chester's limp body into the makeshift sling.

"He's in bad shape," Mr. Nelson said, placing the cat on his wife's lap in the front seat of the car and getting into the driver's seat. The kids piled in the back, leaning over to watch Chester all the way to the vet's.

At the clinic the vet said, "I'm not sure this cat will make it. He's in shock from the trauma and probably has internal injuries. I'll take x-rays and start an intravenous." The door to the examining room closed behind him.

That night the girls slept in Jillian's bed and cried themselves to sleep.

Mrs. Nelson was just getting off the phone when Tanya and Jillian came downstairs early the next morning.

"Chester has no broken bones, but the vet had to operate last night to stop the internal bleeding. We can visit later today."

The girls couldn't eat a thing for breakfast or lunch. They watched the clock until it was time to go. At the clinic, Chester lay on his side in an open cage. He had been cleaned up, but lay completely still with a bandage around his chest.

"It's touch and go right now," the vet said. "Chester hasn't moved since we stitched him up last night."

The girls sat on the floor beside the cage. Jillian leaned close and whispered, "Come on, Chester. You have to live."

"*Zhiví ... zhiví*," Tanya said desperately.

Jillian rubbed gently under Chester's chin and he purred weakly. Tanya stroked behind his ears and Chester's paws twitched.

"See that? It's a good sign. Chester's trying to move toward us," Jillian said.

"He'll have to do more than that," said the vet. "He's not eating and he won't live long unless he does."

"Please let us bring him home," Jillian begged. "Tanya and I can get him to eat."

The vet agreed they could take the cat with them if they promised to keep him calm and undisturbed.

At home they put Chester on a fresh towel in a wicker basket and carried to the kitchen. The girls fed the cat every hour, letting him lick tuna juice from their fingers. They watched Chester struggle to sit up, but his front legs were so weak he'd collapse back onto the towel with every attempt.

"He can't go on like this," Mr. Nelson said.

The next day, the girls soaked cat crumbles in milk and put tiny pieces of the softened pellets into Chester's mouth. He sat for a minute, but couldn't get up on all fours and even though his neck was bent awkwardly to one side, he *did* seem a little better.

The girls stayed by Chester's basket, stroking him

and watching for signs of improvement. To pass the time Tanya taught Jillian to play Cat's Cradle. Together the girls twisted their hands, ducked and looped their fingers. They made Soldier's Bed, Cat's Eye and for their grand finale, the configuration that required four hands, the most challenging trick of them all, The Star.

"See, Chester. *Zvezdá zhelániy*," said Jillian.

Tanya looked so forlorn that Jillian knew her sadness was about more than Chester's accident. Somehow Tanya believed that if Chester didn't get better, Mariana wouldn't either.

Jillian had to believe, for Tanya and for herself, that both Mariana and Chester would recover. "Tanya *maladyéts* for Chester," Jillian said.

"I do good work looking after Chester," Tanya translated.

"Yes, and *dóktor maladyéts* for Mariana," Jillian said, using the Russian words as best she could.

"The doctor is doing good work for Mariana too," Tanya said, tears running down her cheeks.

Jillian scrunched up the bottom of her T-shirt and wiped Tanya's face. "We have to keep believing they'll get better, both of them."

Tanya nodded. "*Zvezdá zhelániy*," she said, looking brighter.

That night Chester took four shaky steps. His neck was still tipped at an angle, but he was making definite progress.

"Looks like this cat's going to make it after all," Dad said.

"Who says cats don't have nine lives?" Jillian joked.

"The cat in the hat came back!" Tanya said triumphantly.

The next day Chester walked slowly, though still not too steadily, across the room.

"He's all better!" Jillian said as she and Tanya prepared to swab his shaved chest with the cream the vet had given them.

Tanya ran her finger lightly over Chester's scar. "*Chernobyl ozherélye*," she said.

"What do you mean 'necklace'?" Jillian asked, puzzled.

"Mama. Chernobyl necklace."

"Your *Máma* has a scar like Chester?"

"Yes. *Máma balná.*"

"Your *Máma* was sick? She had an operation on her neck? Is she still sick?"

"No. *Máma* is well now."

Later, before bed, Jillian told her mother about the Chernobyl necklace.

"I'm not sure what it means, but how terrible that both Tanya's mother and sister have been so ill," her mother said.

Later, from her room, Jillian heard her mother singing to Tanya. She shivered at the thought of her own mother or her father, or David or Gram, getting sick.

Jillian remembered hearing her mother sing that lullaby before. As she listened, feelings from when she was little flooded over her, feelings of love and safety.

She looked over at the photograph of Grandpa in the silver frame and for the first time his memory wasn't shadowy. Jillian was overwhelmed with the tenderness in her grandpa's look.

The next morning another letter came from Tanya's parents. It must have been good news because Tanya couldn't stop smiling. She managed to chew and smile simultaneously while eating grilled cheese and ketchup sandwiches.

Sharon came over to translate the letter: Mariana was home after her first round of treatment and was feeling better. The family had celebrated at dinner with the neighbours. They had picked wild mushrooms in the woods and their *bábushka* had cooked mushroom dumplings. The next day they'd had a picnic by the river and *Pápa* caught a fish. They all missed Tanya very much and didn't want her to worry.

Included was a photograph of the girls' father holding up the fish and one of Mariana. Mariana looked quite well; she wore a red jumper and smiled as she sat on the sofa with her arm around her *bábushka*.

"It is good. I am happy," said Tanya.

"Sharon, I need to ask something," Mrs. Nelson said. "Yesterday Tanya touched Chester's scar and said her mother had a 'Chernobyl necklace'. What does that mean?"

"It's a scar from thyroid surgery," Sharon said. "Probably thyroid cancer. Radioactive iodine from the accident is absorbed by the thyroid gland so it has to be removed. The terrible effects of radioactive fallout go on for years after the accident."

"Tanya's had so much to deal with in her short life," Mr. Nelson said.

"So have all the Belarusian children," Sharon said.

Mrs. Nelson sat with Tanya and Jillian on the front steps. The air was warm and there was a light breeze as they watched the stars sparkle in the night sky.

"I have good news," Jillian's mother said. "Sharon's firm has a vacancy for a mediator this fall. She says she's been impressed with how I managed this summer and she'll recommend me for the job."

"That's awesome," Jillian said. "I guess you'll be glad to get back to work, but thanks for staying home with us this summer. I'm really glad you were here."

"I'm glad, too," her mother answered, leaning over to ruffle her daughter's long hair before heading back into the house.

Jillian moved closer to Tanya on the top step.

"So many stars," Jillian said, looking up. "See the Big Dipper, Tanya?" Jillian pointed. "It looks like a saucepan."

"I see," said Tanya, her head back.

"Now find the two pointer stars on the side. They point to the bright North Star. No matter where you and I are, we'll be looking at the same star in the same place, true north," Jillian said.

Tanya nodded and whispered, "*Zvezdá zhelániy.*"

"Let's think of each other every time we see it."

"I promise," said Tanya, her eyes shining as brightly as any star.

And then, the night air filled with their clear voices:

When you wish upon a star,
Makes no difference who you are,
Anything your heart desires
will come to you.

If your heart is in your dream,
No request is too extreme
When you wish upon a star
as dreamers do.

Like a bolt out of the blue,
Fate steps in and sees you thru,
When you wish upon a star
your dream comes true.

ELEVEN

It was Tanya's last week and her scrapbook was almost full. She'd glued in postcards of the carved wooden grizzly bear at the anthropology museum, a view of the city from the gondola at the top of Grouse Mountain and another of a red pagoda in Chinatown. There were photographs of David in his baseball uniform and of the Canada Day party with everyone waving flags.

Jillian had almost filled her book, too. Her favourite photograph was of the two of them sitting on the beach with the Two Sisters in the background. Below it, Jillian had written: *Tanya and I collected shells at the beach. I showed her the shining inside of the mussel shells. They look so dull and ordinary on the outside — if you didn't look inside them you'd never know how special they really were.*

Tanya had made a little package of beach sand and stuck it in her scrapbook beside a gull's feather. She finished her book with prints of Chester's paw, made by dipping it in red paint and making impressions across the last two pages.

"*Dóbra!*" the girls said to each other.

★

"I have an idea," said Jillian at supper. "Saturday is Tanya's last night. Let's have a party with all the Belarusian kids and their families. A goodbye party!"

"I dunno," said her dad. "I thought it would be nice to have a quiet family dinner. Tanya should be in bed early."

"But Tanya *wants* a party. She loves barbecues, don't you, Tanya?"

"Mark, I love barbecues."

David said, "Are you thinking of inviting all the kids and their sponsors?"

"Yeah. Jasmine and Nina and Sasha …"

"I'll set up the picnic table and the badminton net," David volunteered quickly.

"I'll make a bean salad," Mrs. Nelson said. "Don't forget to invite Sharon."

"I'll phone everyone tonight," Jillian said.

"Okay. Okay. Why not?" her dad agreed. "We'll get salmon at the docks in the morning."

After supper, Jillian got out a list of the hosting families. She'd decided to phone Jasmine last. If Jasmine said, "Sorry, I have a music lesson," the others would already be invited and the party couldn't be cancelled.

Within half an hour Sharon and the first four families had all said yes.

"Will your brother be there?" Nicole asked.

"Sure."

"Good. Should I bring potato salad? I put mustard in the one I make."

"David loves potato salad with mustard," Jillian said, hoping he actually did.

Gram said, "I'll bring a cake. Now that Tanya's eating strawberries again, we can have strawberry shortcake in her honour."

Everything was falling into place. Jillian dialled Jasmine's number.

"It's Jillian Nelson," she said when Jasmine picked up the phone.

"Hiya, Jillian," said Jasmine cheerfully.

When Jillian told her about the barbecue, Jasmine said, "Hey, great idea! We'd love to come. Okay if we bring curried rice? My mother has a good recipe and Nina and I can make it."

"Awesome. See you Saturday!"

When she hung up, Jillian shouted, "They're all coming!" and raced upstairs to tell Tanya.

The next day David handed Tanya a shopping bag. "Sorry it's not wrapped."

"For me?" Tanya asked, pulling out a long, flat tin box. On the cover was a map of the world. Jillian leaned over Tanya's shoulder to read:

> **AROUND THE WORLD IN COLOUR**
> THE WORLD'S LARGEST SET OF FELT PENS
> 72 FABULOUS COLOURS

Inside were rows and rows of felt pens, laid out like coloured piano keys, the names of the colours printed on the side of each one.

"Awesome!" said Tanya.

"She gets that word from you," David said to Jillian.

"It is awesome," Jillian said, giving her brother the 'thumbs-up' sign.

The girls found paper and went to work. Tanya drew a high building with many windows. In front of it she drew flowers in a rainbow of colours — cornflower blue, buttercup yellow, sapphire, violet, hyacinth and cherry red.

"It's my *shkóla*," Tanya said with pride.

In big letters at the bottom of the picture Tanya wrote:

ДЖИЛЛ ОТ ТАНИ
Я ЛЮБЛЮ ТЕБЯ

"This says 'To Jillian from Tanya.'" Tanya pointed to the first line as she handed the picture to Jillian.

"What does it say underneath that?"

Tanya touched her eye.

"Eye."

Tanya placed her hand flat on her chest.

"Heart."

Tanya pointed to Jillian.

"You. Eye heart you!"

Tanya nodded.

"Eye heart you, too, Tanya," Jillian said, grinning.

Jillian bent over her own drawing. "Don't look yet. I'm almost finished."

Tanya said, "Next year in *shkóla* I learn English."

"You'll be the smartest person in your class," Jillian said. "Do you have lots of friends at school?"

"Yes," Tanya said. "You have friends at school?"

Jillian shrugged and was quiet as she finished her drawing. She handed Tanya a picture of a girl about eleven years old with chestnut brown hair, amethyst green eyes and a smile with teeth of alabaster white.

"It's me?" Tanya asked.

Nodding, Jillian said, "You are *krasívaya*. Beautiful."

Tanya shook her head.

"You are!" Jillian said.

"You are *chut-chut smeshnóy*!" said Tanya.

That afternoon Mr. and Mrs. Nelson came home with a parcel for Tanya. Inside was a pair of shiny black shoes with a strap and low heels. In a smaller package was a pair of white socks, rows of lace at the cuffs.

Tanya stared at the gifts. "*Spasíba bolshóy.*"

"It means 'big thanks,'" Jillian told her parents.

Tanya put the shoes on and paraded from one end of the hall to the other. "I love black shoes. I love felt pens, too," she said, smiling at David.

"Great idea to give Tanya those pens, David," Jillian said as the two of them loaded the dishwasher after supper.

"Wish I had an idea about how to talk to a girl my own age," David said.

"Just be natural — joke around the way you do with Tanya and me."

"It doesn't feel natural, but I guess all I can do is try," David said with a grateful smile.

Jillian sat on her bed scratching Chester's neck. It had almost healed, but it itched and Chester rubbed against Jillian's hand to remind her to scratch.

"Got any ideas, Chester?"

Everyone but Jillian had given Tanya a present. Her present had to be something *really* special. But she didn't have any money and she didn't have any ideas. Not one. And there was just tomorrow left. Jillian rubbed one side of Chester's neck. Then the other.

Suddenly she jumped off the bed and Chester fell to the floor. She had it! The perfect gift for Tanya!

★

Early the next morning the girls went to the Steveston docks with Mr. Nelson. Tanya wore her new black shoes and the heels clicked smartly as she paraded along the wharf where the trawlers were moored. The fishers held up salmon from the hold of their boats and, after inspecting each and every one, Mr. Nelson eventually chose a big twelve-pounder that pleased him. The fish was wrapped in newspaper and they headed back to town.

Jillian was waiting at the front door when Gram drove up a few hours later.

"I have to talk to you, Gram," she said. "Privately."

"Okay. Let me put this cake down first."

They disappeared to Jillian's bedroom for half an hour and when they returned to the kitchen, Mr. Nelson asked, "So what's the big deal?"

"It's a secret," Jillian said.

"A big one too," said Gram.

"Secrets, secrets. I'm curious," said Jillian's mother, arriving with Tanya, both of them carrying boxes of fresh strawberries.

"Can't tell you, Mum."

"Tell me?" Tanya asked.

"Sorry, Tanya. *Bolshóy, bolshóy sekrét.*"

"Give us a hint?" her dad asked.

"Wait 'til Tanya's gone home."

"Seems hard to believe she leaves tomorrow morning," said Mrs. Nelson.

Gram took a parcel from her bag. "I've got something for you, Tanya," she said. Gram had made a soft fleece jacket the colour of apricots.

"It's for those cold winters in Belarus," Gram said.

"Thank you, *Bába*. I love it too much." Tanya kissed Gram, first on one cheek, then on the other.

"And here's one for Mariana." Gram handed Tanya a jacket the colour of ripe plums.

"Mariana will love it too much," Tanya said.

By four o'clock everyone was ready.

David wore his favourite soccer shirt. Tanya and Jillian wore matching red halter-tops and shorts. Jillian had watched Tanya smile at herself in the mirror, turning to see the back of her hair, running her hand over her face, then bending both arms to flex her muscles.

Jasmine and Nina and Mr. and Mrs. Sandhu arrived first, Jasmine carrying a large bowl of curried rice.

The girls rushed to play badminton in the back yard.

After a few bad serves, Jillian said to Jasmine, "Sorry, I'm not much good at this."

"We can practise together some time, if you like," Jasmine said.

"Sure," Jillian said, hardly able to believe her ears.

Just then, Nicole and her mother and Sasha arrived, quickly followed by the other families with their Belarusian guests.

David carried Sasha around the yard on his shoulders and the others played tag and badminton. When Tanya and Jillian did cartwheels, holding up their arms like gymnasts when they finished, all the guests applauded.

Lyn Nelson and Sharon looked at each other and smiled.

The salmon was a great success and everyone asked for the marinade recipe. When it was time for dessert, David offered to get shortcake for Nicole and said, "Could I get you some of my special sauce to go with the strawberries?"

"Don't you dare play a trick on me, David Nelson!" Nicole said.

"What? A nice guy like me?" David said with a grin.

Nicole flipped her hair over her shoulder and grinned back.

Later, David led Tanya to the front of the crowd. "Just like we practised," he whispered in her ear.

"Knock, knock," said Tanya in a loud voice.

"Well, who's there?" asked Mr. Nelson.

"Want."

"Want who?"

"Wan-two-three-four-joke!" came Tanya's confident reply.

The crowd laughed and clapped. Tanya looked around, beaming.

Then Sharon said a few words. "I want to thank all the host families for welcoming these children into your homes. I know at times it hasn't been easy, but there is no doubt this summer has made a big difference in their lives. Don't lose touch with each other. And remember, I'll be available to translate letters and e-mail messages."

Jasmine's mother turned to Mrs. Nelson and said,

"I worry that most of the world has forgotten about Belarus."

Lyn Nelson shook her head. "What we've done is so small in comparison to what's needed."

"Maybe the best we can do is help one child at a time," Amrit Sandhu said. "This summer has made a real difference to Nina. And Sasha looks much healthier too."

"Tanya has lots of energy and she's wearing clothes a size larger than when she arrived," said Jillian's mother.

Mrs. Sandhu said, "Doctors say that a child's health improves greatly if they come back for two or three summers."

"That's a good idea," said Jillian's mother.

As the children from Belarus were leaving they called, " *Spasíba. Paká. Paká.*"

David walked Nicole to the car. "Great potato salad."

"*Paká*," she said with a wink.

Gram and Jillian were packing the car. Gram whispered in her granddaughter's ear, "I'll be thinking about our secret tomorrow."

When it was just the Sandhus and the Nelsons left, Jasmine said to Jillian, "I really had fun."

"Me too," Jillian said.

"I'm glad we'll be in the same class again next year."

"Wonder if Ross is still wearing his baseball cap backward?" Jillian said.

"We'll soon find out!" Jasmine laughed.

★

Two packed suitcases lay open on Tanya's bed, both of them full to the brim. In one lay neatly folded clothes — jeans, skirts, T-shirts and pyjamas for Tanya and Mariana. Its corners overflowed with toothbrushes, toothpaste, vitamin pills and writing paper.

In the second suitcase, three bottles of ketchup were tucked inside a winter jacket for Mariana and beside it sat the large tin box of felt pens. Stuffed inside warm wool socks for Tanya's parents was a collection of Vancouver beach shells. The big scrapbook was the last to go in.

As the girls sat, one on each lid, to close the suitcases, Jillian said to Tanya, "I think I *will* have friends at school next year. I'll be seeing Jasmine a lot and I figure if she likes Gail and Molly, they can't be all that bad. I really need to ask Molly about braces and I'm going to invite Jasmine and Ross over to play badminton."

Tanya smiled; she could see her *druk* was happy. The girls lugged the suitcases down to the front door where the rest of the family waited. Mr. Woodman had been cutting his lawn and came over to say goodbye.

"How about taking a group photo for us?" Jillian's mom asked, handing her camera to Mr. Woodman.

Mr. and Mrs. Nelson sat on the top step, David sprawled one step below, and the two girls leaned against each other on the bottom step. Tanya was holding Chester and Jillian held the star wand in the air. They were laughing because instead of, "Say cheese," Tanya had said, "Say *syr*."

"Have a good trip home, Tanya," Mr. Woodman said.

"Home is good," Tanya answered.

"Yes, home is good," Jillian agreed.

In the driveway, Tanya said a sad goodbye to Chester, cradling him in her arms and nuzzling her face into his fur as she whispered, "*Kótik, kótik.*"

"That cat's starting to meow with an accent," David said as he and Jillian sat on either side of Tanya in the back seat. Jillian kept her legs pressed against a red bag.

Inside the airport, the children from Belarus gathered with their Canadian families. Nina and Sasha were huddled closely together. Jillian and David waved at them, then at Jasmine and Nicole.

"We'll miss you," Mrs. Nelson, said smiling at Tanya, who had tears running down her cheeks.

"Oh, Tanya, don't cry," she said as her own eyes filled.

David's voice was croakier than ever. "Don't forget to brush your teeth, Tanya. You've got to keep that great smile."

Mr. Nelson picked Tanya up in his arms, swung her in the air and said, "Next summer you'll be too big for me to do this."

Next summer!

Then it was Jillian's turn to say goodbye. "I'm excited for you because you're going home, but sad because you're leaving us."

Tanya was crying, but she managed to say, "Excited. Sad."

"Remember our wishing star."

"I remember."

Tanya looked at the family and struggled to find the words she needed. "I not forget you. Thank you."

"You-are-welcome," said the Nelsons.

"*Paká, druk,*" Jillian said quietly. "See you next year."

She pointed to her eye, laid her hand on her heart and pointed to her friend. They hugged each other long and hard.

Tanya joined the other children and was the last of the group at the departure gate. When she reached up to wipe her cheeks, Jillian realized the red bag was still in her hand. She ran to catch up to Tanya.

"For you and Mariana," she said, handing her the bag.

The family watched as Tanya turned. Holding the bag in one hand, she raised the other arm, the arm with four friendship bracelets, in a big wave.

On the drive home, Jillian's mother asked, "What was in the red bag, Jillian?"

"Well, I knew that Tanya loved the music box the first moment she saw it," Jillian began.

There was a hush in the car.

"So I talked to Gram and she said the music box was mine and I could do whatever I wanted with it."

Jillian took a breath. "I asked Gram if she had something to remind her of Grandpa and she said that all she needed was the feeling in her heart. Now I have that feeling about Grandpa too."

Nobody said a word.

"Gram agreed that Tanya and Mariana need the music box more than I do."

Jillian's parents exchanged a glance and David did something surprising. He reached over and put his arm on Jillian's shoulders.

"You know, you're not a bad kid. For a sister. If you keep this up you might just get a box of felt pens for your birthday," he said.

"Seventy-two?"

"Could be."

"In a box that says AROUND THE WORLD IN COLOUR?"

"Wait and see."

"You're not so bad either. For a brother." Jillian stretched up and kissed her brother on one cheek and then, to his astonishment, on the other.

"Russian kiss!" she said.

David leaned away. "Cut that out! If I need slobber I'll get a dog."

"Or a girlfriend!" said Jillian, laughing so hard that everyone in the car joined in.

With a little flip of her hair, Jillian sat back contentedly onto the seat. As they approached the city, she could see across the bay to where the sun flashed off the peaks of The Sisters.

The summer was over and she had a friend. Tanya

lived half a world away, it was true, but soon Jillian knew she'd have a friend in Vancouver, too.

When they turned the corner and started up the hill, Jillian said, "I've promised to write to Tanya and tell her all about school. It's going to be an awesome year!"

Mr. Nelson pulled the car into the driveway and Jillian realized her dad had been right. They *had* seen the world from the wide steps of the house on the hill.

GLOSSARY OF RUSSIAN WORDS

Since 1995, Belarus, like Canada, has had two official languages: Belarusian and Russian. Like most children in Belarus, Tanya understands both languages. These words have been transliterated from the Russian Cyrillic alphabet, which means they have been spelled the way they sound in English so you can pronounce them. A stroke (/) is placed over the part of the word that is stressed. You say that part more strongly.

Russian to English

azyóra	lakes
bábushka	grandmother
balná	sick
blúzka	blouse
bolsháya	big (f)
bolshóy	big (m)

chut-chut	little bit
da	yes
da svidániya	goodbye
den razhdéniya	birthday
dóbra	good work
	(Tanya says this in Belarusian)
dóktor	doctor
dom	house
druk	friend
dva	two
flamáster	felt pens
frúkty	fruit
góry	mountains
i	and
Kanáda	Canada
kot	cat
kótik	little cat
krasívaya	beautiful
kravát	bed (cradle)
maladyéts	doing good work
malakó	milk
máma	mother
mashína	car
ménshe	smaller
múzyka	music
nyet	no
ozherélye	necklace
paká	see you/bye
pápa	father
pazhálusta	please

pisát	write
pismó	letter
privét	hello
sekrét	secret
serébryaniye beryózy	silver birch trees
shkóla	school
smeshnóy	funny
spasíba	thank you
syóstry	sisters
syr	cheese
túfli	shoes
yógurt	yoghurt
zhiví	live
zvezdá zhelániy	wishing star

English to Russian

and	*i*
beautiful	*krasívaya*
bed (cradle)	*kravát*
big	*bolshóy (m)/bolsháya (f)*
birthday	*den razhdéniya*
blouse	*blúzka*
Canada	*Kanáda*
car	*mashína*
cat	*kot/kótik (little cat)*
cheese	*syr*
doctor	*dóktor*
doing good work	*maladyéts*
father	*pápa*
felt pens	*flamáster*

friend	*druk*
fruit	*frúkty*
funny	*smeshnóy*
good work/well done	*dobra*
	(Tanya says this in Belarusian)
goodbye	*da svidániya*
grandmother	*bábushka*
hello	*privét*
house	*dom*
lakes	*azyóra*
letter	*pismó*
little bit	*chut-chut*
live	*zhiví*
milk	*malakó*
mother	*máma*
mountains	*góry*
music	*múzyka*
necklace	*ozherélye*
no	*nyet*
please	*pazhálusta*
school	*shkóla*
secret	*sekrét*
see you/bye	*paká*
shoes	*túfli*
sick	*balná*
silver birch trees	*serébryaniye beryózy*
sisters	*syóstry*
smaller	*ménshe*
star	*zvezdá*
thank you	*spasíba*

two	*dva*
wishing star	*zvezdá zhelániy*
write	*pisát*
yes	*da*
yoghurt	*yógurt*

Once called White Russia (Belorussiya), Belarus was part of the USSR until 1991. It is now an independent country with a population of 10.3 million.

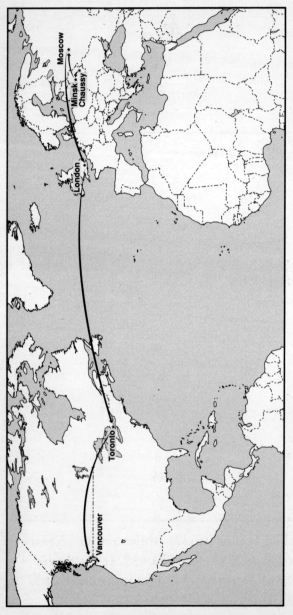

Tanya travelled over 12,000 kilometres, by bus from Chaussy to Minsk, then by plane to Moscow, London, Toronto and Vancouver.

ACKNOWLEDGMENTS

I want to acknowledge my enormous gratitude to Tom Blom for his inspiration, imagination and generous support as he showed me how to make this story work.

I would also like to thank: Olive Johnson, Shelley Hrdlitschka, Dianne Woodman, Ellen Schwartz, Norma Charles, Maureen Bayless, Anne Fraser, Suzanne Norman, Ann-Marie Metten, Margot Young and Joy Gugeler for helpful editing guidance; Bonny Cyr and the children in her 1998/99 class at General Gordon School; Lisa Stevenson, Emma Ingebietsen, and Eli and Hannah Leyland for reading the manuscript; Madeleine Nelson, Alison Jancy, Cindy Van Nerum, Maureen Thackeray, Lyn LeBlanc, Jeannie Bates, Louise Hager, Sharon Kahn, Dr. Janette Craven and Jeremy Young for research assistance; Regina

Lyakhovetska, Joanna Survilla, Galina Moushtaler, Elena Urbanovich and Pavel Shidlovsky for help with transliteration from Russian and Belarusian; and the courageous children from Belarus who taught me about trust and hope in our uncertain world.

Wishing Star Summer is a fictionalized story based on the experiences of generous Canadian families who have opened their doors and their hearts to the children of Belarus. For more information contact:

Canadian Relief Fund for Chernobyl Victims
in Belarus
190 Bronson Avenue
Ottawa, Ontario
Canada K1R 6H4
Telephone: (613) 567-9595
Fax: (613) 567-9971
E-mail: crfcvb@cyberus.ca
Web: www.crfcvb.ca

BERYL YOUNG has published articles, poetry and translations in Canadian magazines and journals and has appeared on CBC radio and television. In 1995 she was writer-in-residence at Wallace Stegner House in Saskatchewan and in 1997 held the same position at the Wurlitzer Foundation for the Arts in New Mexico. Young has produced recordings for children, including one that went on to become a gold record (50,000 copies). Young has a foster child in India she visits regularly and spends part of each winter volunteering in Central America. She has three children and three grand-children. Her youngest son has hosted visitors from Belarus since 1997. She lives in Vancouver.

Other Raincoast YA Fiction:

The Accomplice by Norma Charles
1-55192-430-7 $9.95 CDN $6.95 US

In Charles' ninth book, twelve-year-old Megan and her younger sister Jen agree to meet their estranged father for a secret reunion, but when he takes them to his island cabin to meet his new wife and child, Megan begins to suspect that she has been an unwitting accomplice to a scheme that threatens them all.

Cat's Eye Corner by Terry Griggs
1-55192-350-5 $9.95 CDN $6.95 US

When Olivier visits his grandfather, retired to Cat's Eye Corner with a reported witch, he finds himself on a strange scavenger hunt in the Dark Wood. Soon he is knee-deep in adventures with the So-So Gang, a talking pen, a girl named Linnett who controls the wind and mischievous word fairies called Inklings.

Dead Reckoning by Julie Burtinshaw
1-55192-342-4 $9.95 CDN $6.95 US

Fourteen-year-old James boards the steamship *Valencia* in San Francisco's harbour in 1906 unprepared for the violent storm that forces the crew to rely on dead reckoning. When the vessel runs aground in seas too rocky for rescue James and his friend Alex board the last lifeboat …

Raven's Flight by Diane Silvey
1-55192-344-0 $9.95 CDN $6.95 US

In Silvey's fourth book, fifteen-year-old Raven searches for her missing sister, Marcie, reportedly "working" in Vancouver's downtown east side. But when Raven learns that Marcie is wanted by a kidnapping ring abducting children to be smuggled across the Pacific, Raven must put together clues from Marcie's diary before it's too late.